Ω

Death Sentence

BOOKS BY
Brian Garfield

Brian Wynne Garfield

Ω

DEATH SENTENCE

A NOVEL

M. Evans and Company, Inc.
New York, New York 10017

M. Evans and Company titles are distributed in
the United States by the J. B. Lippincott Company,
East Washington Square, Philadelphia, Pa. 19105;
and in Canada by McClelland & Stewart Ltd.,
25 Hollinger Road, Toronto M4B 3G2, Ontario

LIBRARY OF CONGRESS CATALOGING IN PUBLICATION DATA

Garfield, Brian Wynne, 1939-
Death sentence.

I. Title.
PZ4.G2315Db   [PS3557.A715]   813'.5'4   75-20031
ISBN 0-87131-198-4

Design by Joel Schick

Manufactured in the United States of America

9 8 7 6 5 4 3 2 1

Lost is our old simplicity of times;
The world abounds with laws,
and teems with crimes

Pennsylvania Gazette,
Feb. 8, 1775.

With ready-made opinions one
cannot judge of crime.
Its philosophy is a little more
complicated than people think.
It is acknowledged that
neither convict prisons
nor any system of hard labor
ever cured a criminal.

FYODOR DOSTOIEVSKY
The House of the Dead

Ω

1

THE GUNS pointed in every direction. They were strewn under glass and Paul Benjamin went the length of the counter studying them.

"Interested in handguns?"

The proprietor was hopeful not so much for a sale as for conversation. Paul recognized the inquisitive tone—guns were objects of beauty, artifacts; give the proprietor encouragement and he'd wheel out his display of flintlocks from a back room.

The shop was heavy with oiled rifles and shotguns. Here and there a decorative sword; one corner grudgingly displayed fishing tackle; all the rest was guns.

The proprietor dragged a lame foot when he walked: perhaps his passion for firearms came from their lack of human imperfection. He had grey skin and little moist eyes and an apologetic smile. A recluse. If it weren't guns it would be a meticulous array of electric trains in his basement. Evidently he was Truett; that was the name painted on the front window.

Under the buzzing fluorescent tubes Paul's hand looked veined and pale. "Could I see that one?"

"The Webley?" Truett unlocked the back of the case.

"No—next to it. The thirty-eight?"

"This one you mean. The automatic."

"Yes."

"Smith and Wesson." Truett put it on top of the case. "You know the weapon?"

"No. . . ."

Truett slid a blotter cloth along the glass and overturned the pistol on it. "Takes your standard nine-millimeter round." He popped the magazine out of the handle and proffered the pistol.

Paul took it tentatively.

The ball of Truett's thumb massaged the side of the empty magazine. "A gun ought to be selected for its use. You mind if I ask what purpose you have in mind?"

Paul had the lie ready: it was glib on his tongue. "I've just moved out from New Jersey. My brother and I bought a radio and electronics shop down in Chicago. We're opening next week."

"You want a gun under the counter against holdups, then."

"We thought of buying two guns. A very small one that would fit in the back of the cash-register drawer, and a bigger one to keep under the counter."

"Makes sense. Crime what it is today. . . ." Truett retrieved the pistol and slid the magazine into it. "You don't want this one."

"No?"

"Maybe you'll have kids wandering around the shop. You'd have to leave the chamber empty and the safety engaged. By the time you got it loaded and off safety the holdup men could shoot you fourteen times. Look here."

Paul watched him grip the slide with his left hand.

"Assume that's a loaded magazine I just inserted. Here's what you've got to do before you can fire this thing. It takes two hands and it can't be done silently."

Truett pulled the slide back. There was a metallic racket when springs shot it home.

"Now you've loaded a cartridge into the chamber and you've cocked the weapon. But you've still got to push the safety off with your thumb, like so." Truett aimed the pistol at a wall. "*Now* you're ready to shoot."

He put it away under the glass. "Single-action automatic is not a good defense weapon. You want a good revolver, or a double-action automatic."

"I see."

"Now here's a manstopper." Truett's voice was different. He lifted something from the case and held it flat on his palms like a reverential offering.

It had the beauty of extraordinary ugliness.

"Too bad it's got the same disadvantages as that other automatic. But this is a collector's item—I'll lay odds you've never seen a Luger like this one. They only made a handful of these in forty-five caliber."

Paul tried to put a polite show of interest on his face to mask his fascination. The .45 Luger had ugly lines: bulging tumors of dark steel. He felt mesmerized.

"A crook finds something like this pointed at his face, he might just faint from fear without you having to shoot at all." Truett smiled but the smile was awry with unexpected cruelty. Paul stared at the Luger when Truett aimed it carefully past him into neutral shadows. It was like staring into the orifice of a cannon.

"Far as I know this is the only one like it this side of Los

Angeles. Forty-five Lugers are like hen's teeth." Truett looked as if he wanted to caress it. "But you don't want a piece like this for shop protection." He put it away under the glass with great care; then he moved away. "I think I've got what you want. Somewhere here. . . ."

Paul stood above the Luger and talked himself out of it. It was slow and it was too bulky, and above all it was noticeable. He needed something the reverse. Something anonymous, easily concealed, fast to use—a tree in a forest, untraceable because it was identical with ten thousand others. One like the gun he'd left behind in New York. A gun for killing.

He was thinking: I'm an ordinary middle-aged product of a middle-class life. Just like everybody else—born innocent and taught cowardice at an early age. We live our lives in fear. Only this thing has happened in me and I can't accept that any more. They killed my daughter and my wife. And I'm here buying a gun because I will not be afraid of them any more. I'm a madman, or I'm the only sane man. And who's to decide that?

Today he would buy the gun and tonight in the city he would hunt. It wasn't the fever of a holy mission; he didn't feel obsessed by any sort of fanaticism and it wasn't pleasure to think about it. But it was something that ought to be done. To rid the streets of them so that perhaps the next man's daughter might be spared. There was no joy in it: if you were a doctor you didn't enjoy jabbing needles into people; but Carol and Esther were dead for all time and he had a duty to them.

Truett had found a cardboard box lined with crumpled crepe; fitted into it was a stubby revolver glossy with new blackness.

"Smith and Wesson Centennial. Five shots, hammerless,

grip safety, compact, light, takes the thirty-eight special cartridge. Two-inch barrel, tapered sight and shrouded hammer to keep from snagging on your pocket or drawer. This is just about the safest revolver they make, in terms of leaving it loaded around small children. It can't be fired unless it's held in a proper grip, you see, you've got to squeeze the handle as well as the trigger. It can't go off if it drops on the floor. I'd recommend this one."

Paul tried it in his hand. It was as weightless as a child's toy gun. He dredged a phrase from somewhere in his experience: "What about stopping power?"

"It's the standard police cartridge. Of course you wouldn't want to try long-range stunts with it, not with that short barrel, but a good shooter can hit a man thirty feet away with one of these pocket guns and that's the longest you'd need inside a shop. It kicks like a mule, being so lightweight, but I guess you'd rather have a sore hand than a knife or a bullet in you. Now this is only a five-shot revolver, not a six-shooter, but that makes it less bulky and the piece can handle heavy powder loads because the bolt-cuts don't come over the centers of the chambers. It means you can use high-speed ammunition, next thing to magnum load."

Truett went down the counter and found a box. There was a small flat pistol inside. Paul had seen something like it on a desk once and it had turned out to be a cigarette lighter.

"I recommend these for cash-register drawers. It's only a twenty-five caliber auto, but hollow-point loads are your answer and you've got to figure you'd only use it at point-blank range anyway. You'd still have to hit a vital spot to kill a man but a hollow-point would chew him up pretty badly wherever it hit him." Truett talked dispassionately and it was possible his expertise about anatomical damage

5

came from articles in gun periodicals: he didn't look as if he had ever shot a human being. *But then I don't suppose I do either.*

"They say a real hard case would rather get drilled by a three fifty-seven magnum than by one of these with hollow-points. A big gun's likely to shoot straight through you and leave a clean hole. One of these doesn't pack enough power to go all the way through cartilage. You get one of these little bullets stuck in the middle of you and you're liable to die from the sepsis unless you get it removed and cleaned out by a good surgeon. A man who knows his guns will respect one of these when he finds it aimed at him."

Truett set the .25 toy beside the revolver and found boxes of ammunition. "Soft-nose hollow-points. They used to call them dum-dums—know why? They were originally made in a town in India called Dum-Dum. These bullets literally explode inside the body."

"I'll want a few more boxes. For practice. My brother and I ought to go out and get the feel of these guns, I think. If we ever have to use them we'd better be familiar with them."

"That's always a good idea. Whereabouts is your shop?"

He had to think quickly. He didn't know Chicago yet; he'd only just arrived. He remembered the place where he'd bought the secondhand car: the row of car dealers and store-fronts. "Along Western Avenue," he said. "Just south of the Evanston line."

"I get a lot of customers like you. Haven't been in Illinois long enough to qualify for a firearm owner's identification card, so they come across the line here into Wisconsin. Silly damned law—anybody at all can get the permit but it's got that idiotic residency requirement. But I can't complain—it's been good for my business up here. Anyhow there's half a million *licensed* handguns in Chicago. Who do they think they're kidding?" Truett rummaged in the drawer and lifted out several boxes of cartridges. "If you know anybody in business on the North Side you might inquire about getting a guest membership at the Lincoln Park Gun Club. That's on Lake Shore Drive not far from your shop."

"Thanks. I'll ask around."

The .38 Centennial was a perfect pocket gun, he thought; it was small and it was clean with no jagged protuberances to catch on cloth. The tiny flat automatic could be hidden nearly anywhere—ideal for emergency reinforcement. It was a refinement that had occurred to him recently: what if the gun failed? He had to have a second gun.

"Anything else I can help you with?"

"No thanks. Wrap them up."

7

Ω
―――――――――――

2

HE HAD TO fill out forms: Federal registration of the two guns. He'd anticipated it and the driver's license he showed Truett wasn't his own. It was a New Jersey license that had been among his late brother-in-law's effects and the three-year license still had two months to go before its expiration. Anyone who traced either of the guns to Robert Neuser of Piermont Road in Tenafly would find a dead end.

He carried the parcel out to his three-year-old Pontiac and placed it on the seat beside the gun-cleaning kit he'd brought with him from New York. He turned the key and backed out of the parking space; it was starting to rain.

It was one of the small towns that had been by-passed by the new Interstate expressways, abandoned by travelers and left to wither: the motels needed paint and announced their vacancies hopelessly; a roadside diner had been boarded up.

It was a warm day for winter but the leafless trees were

bleak against grey skies. Christmas buntings sagged across the street. He drove through the center of town and followed the patched road east. It two-laned across prairie farms and brought him at four o'clock to a ramp that merged into the southbound Interstate. He was across the line into Illinois in fifteen minutes' time and the rush-hour headlights swarmed in the opposite lanes by the time he crossed the suburb boundary between Lincolnwood and Chicago, wipers batting away the drizzle. He was trying to forget the things that had made him shriek.

He left the rain behind at the end of the expressway and drove aimlessly, not quite sure where he was until he passed the Water Tower and the John Hancock skyscraper and the Continental Plaza where he'd stayed his first two nights in Chicago; he made a turn and went along some one-way street to Lake Shore Drive and rolled south with the high-rises on his right. But when he reached the turn-off for his apartment building he went on by; he didn't want to go home yet. He drove past the lights of the Loop. It was time to have his first look at the South Side.

He drove slowly and impatient cars flashed past him in the outside lanes. There were flat patches of darkness between him and the city. Swamps? Railroad yards? Parks? In the night he couldn't tell. He stopped at a traffic light and when it changed he made a right turn on Balbo and found himself in the Loop: he'd left the Drive too soon. He jigged left and found himself in a tangle of dead ends butting against the railway switching yards.

On impulse he parked in a side street. It was a district of daytime commerce: everything was shut down and there were few lights. No one walked the curbs.

He unwrapped the parcel and loaded the guns. The Centennial went into his topcoat pocket; the flat .25 automatic into his hip pocket, no bigger nor heavier than a wallet. He put the cleaning kit and the boxes of ammunition under the font seat and locked the car when he got out.

The old rage simmered in him. At street corners he stopped and studied the signs, trying to memorize the intersections: he wanted to learn the city. Holden, Plymouth, Federal, LaSalle. Near the intersection of Michigan and Roosevelt he saw a long covered pedestrian bridge across the rail yards, high in the air and walled with glass. Tall covered stairs at either end gave access to it: a good place for a trap, he thought. He watched for ten minutes. If an innocent entered the trap would a predator follow? The interior of the bridge was visible from the street but the lighting was dim and there were deep shadows between overhead lamps where two or three of them had burned out: the dark places where they liked to accost a mark. At the end of the ten minutes a man in working clothes entered the western staircase and Paul watched him appear at the top and make his long pilgrimage across the bridge but nothing interrupted the solitary journey and afterward Paul moved on, the damp wind biting his ears.

Esther. . . . Carol. . . .

By eight he was back in the car driving south and the quality of the city changed with each block until he was in the ghetto. Funeral Home. Pool Hall. Social Club. Liquors. Cut-Rate Discount. Jesus Saves. He turned off the boulevard and rolled along a residential street parallel to it: three-story tenements, wooden fire-escape stairs hanging from their walls. Young dark people lounged under the street lamps and stared at his car as he crept past. *Come on. Come at me.* But they only watched, their insolence muted by motionlessness, and he had to drive on.

He made a right turn into a wide boulevard. A bus swished past; there wasn't much other traffic. He cruised west and the ghetto changed. Soul Food gave way to Tacos and Bodegas. He stopped at a red light and rolled the window down. An El train clattered faintly in the distance; from a bar came the juke-box thumpings of Spanish music. A souped-up car with enormous rear tires growled past him like a mutant insect. In the next block he parked, hungry, and went into a café and ate at the counter: he had discovered Mexican food in Arizona, where he'd got his first gun.

The Centennial was a familiar weight in his coat pocket; he'd felt vulnerable the past few days, empty-pocketed in the city.

The *chili relleno* was good; he washed it down with beer. He paid the fat woman and went back to the street. It was coming up on nine o'clock and getting colder. A Christmas banner across a drugstore said *"Feliz Navidad"* and three laughing men came out of a bar, one of them carrying a six-pack.

He got back in the car frustrated: he didn't know the city well enough. He drove in any direction, prowling.

He had no idea where he was but there was a map in the glove compartment and eventually he'd consult it and find his way home; in the meantime he had to explore.

It was a bar on a dark street somewhere a bit north and west of the center of things: through the window it looked like a boisterous drunk crowd and not far down the street two men in shabby coats sat on porch steps watching the bar. Paul had only a glimpse of them when he drove past but it was as if he read their thoughts and when he reached the corner he turned out of their sight and searched for a place to park the car. He found a spot a block away and locked the doors and circled the block on foot; he stopped at the corner and waited while several cars drove by. When he looked past the corner he saw the front of the bar and if he stepped out a pace he could see the two young men on the stoop; he did it once and then faded back because he didn't want to alert them. They were still sitting there, passing a bottle back and forth between them—probably wine. But they were young and wiry under the tattered coats and the immobility of their features had given them away to him instantly: he knew them, he'd made a study of their kind and Chicago was no different from New York when it came to that subspecies.

He fixed the plan in his head and then stepped out into plain sight on the curb. He walked as if he were a little drunk; he didn't exaggerate it but he moved with slow deliberate care, a bit owlish, not staggering. He looked both ways and crossed the street briskly and tripped over the curb mounting the sidewalk; he made a show of gathering his dignity and went into the bar. He hadn't had to look at the two men on the stoop to know they'd been watching him.

There was a loud crush of celebrants. They were in shabby booths and three-deep at the bar. It was a plain saloon, at least fifty years old by the look of it and unchanged from its origins except for the blown-up photographic posters on the walls: Brendan Behan and Eugene O'Neill and someone whose face Paul didn't recognize— probably an Irish Republican patriot from the 1920s; the room dripped with Irish accents and there was no mistaking the lilt of the ebullient shouts that exploded from the knot of fat men at the far end of the bar. A barmaid in a red wig elbowed past him with a tray of beers.

He stationed himself near the window where the two men across the street could see his back. He ordered ginger ales and drank them quickly, three in succession, and was buttonholed by two loudmouths who demanded that he settle an argument about Catfish Hunter. He pleaded ignorance and was flooded immediately with information or misinformation about baseball. When he judged enough time had passed he went back through the crowd, waited his turn and relieved himself in the men's room. He washed the sweat off his hands and threaded his way to the front door fighting down the fear inside him: he waved drunkenly to his two conversational companions and lurched outside, all but colliding with a laughing couple on their way in.

He looked one way and then the other, a man drunk enough to have trouble remembering where he'd parked his car. Sweat slicked his palms and he rubbed them on the cloth inside his coat pockets. He started off in the wrong direction, brought himself up with anger and stumbled back toward the corner.

In the edge of his vision the two young men on the stoop sat up a bit. Their hats turned, indicating their interest in his progress.

Paul stopped at the corner and studied all four streets in turn with the great concentration of the inebriate: then he stepped carefully off the curb and weaved toward the far side, maintaining his balance with visible effort.

Inside the drunk's act he was afraid. *You don't have to try it. You don't have to die. Don't come after me.*

But the fear was on his tongue. It was familiar terror, an old acquaintance, a frightening thing compounded of their intentions and his own: he was afraid of them but afraid of himself as well, afraid of what he knew he would do. It was something he sensed but still did not understand.

He knew they wouldn't leave him alone. They'd had that bar staked out for hours waiting for a mark like him; they wouldn't get a better shot if they waited a week. A lone drunk lurching into a dark street trying to remember where he'd parked hs car. . . .

He breathed deeply and regularly to calm himself. Into shadow now and he stopped on the edge of the curb pretending anger because he couldn't find his car. He had his back to them but he knew they were there because their silhouettes obscured the splash of streetlight when they reached the corner.

He stooped and tried to fit his key into the door of a car but it was the wrong car and he swore an oath—loud enough to reach the two men's ears—and gave the offending car a petulant kick and went on, bending down to peer close at each parked car he passed.

When they came for him they came in a rush and one of them had the wine bottle upraised, ready to strike at the back of Paul's skull; the other had a folding knife opened to rip upward with the extended blade.

He heard them in plenty of time but the fear paralyzed him momentarily; he moved slower than he should have— he didn't know the gun yet, he should have allowed more time, but they were nearly on top of him when he crouched and turned, stretching his arm out.

It stopped them in their tracks. They had a good look at his undrunk eyes and the black revolver: they knew what hit them.

The noise was intense, earsplitting; the gun crashed against the heel of his hand.

The man with the wine bottle bent double. Paul shifted his aim and shot the knife man in the chest.

He barely heard the bottle shatter on the pavement. He shot both men in the heads while they were falling because they had to be dead so that they couldn't identify him.

In a chilly sweat of terror he staggered away.

Ω
_____

3

HE RACKED the Pontiac into its stall in the underground garage. The attendant was in uniform and armed with a revolver in a holster; Paul greeted him and took the elevator straight up to his floor, the seventeenth.

It was a high-rise, 501 Lake Shore Drive, an apartment tower at the T-end of Grand Avenue. Spalter had tried to steer him to a suburban real-estate agent but Paul had spent his life in apartments except for one brief attempt to live in a house and in the end he had found Number 501 in a classified ad in the real-estate section of the Sunday *Tribune* and he'd taken the apartment the same afternoon.

The steel door had the ordinary slip lock and a dead bolt above. He had to use two keys to let himself in. Behind him closed-circuit TV eyes guarded the corridor. He shut the door and turned both locks before he switched on the lamps and put down his parcel on the coffee table.

He had taken it furnished on a sublet; he wasn't sure

how long he'd stay. The furniture was functional and as characterless as that of a hotel room; the lease tenant was an English instructor at the University of Chicago who was spending a sabbatical in London and who evidently was indifferent to the style of his physical surroundings; the only feature that suggested anything about its previous occupant was the long wall of floor-to-ceiling bookcases, most of them empty now. There were a living room and a bedroom and the kitchenette alcove. The windows looked out on the Loop and that meant it was a less expensive flat than the ones across the hall which commanded views of Lake Michigan and the Navy Pier. Nevertheless this was the Gold Coast and the rent was high by any standards except those of New York.

He drew the blinds before he took out the two guns and put them on the coffee table; then he hung his topcoat in the hall closet and made himself a drink from the refrigerator before he sat down and opened the parcel, got out the cleaning kit and unloaded the Centennial and performed the routine that had become mindless habit in his New York apartment. In an obscure way it made him feel at home in this room for the first time. He broke the revolver's cylinder open to the side, threaded a cloth patch through the needle's eye at the tip of the ramrod, dipped it in solvent until it was soaking and then ran it through the open barrel of the revolver. It came out stained with black gunpowder residue and he had to soak several patches and run them through before one came out clean. He swabbed all five chambers of the cylinder and then ran an oil-soaked patch through the clean orifices to coat them and protect them from corrosion. He oiled the mechanism with the needle-point oilcan and put the kit back together, loaded the revolver and then mopped up the table's glass top.

He'd be safe carrying the guns on his person for a few

days; after that they'd start looking for him and he'd have to find a place away from the apartment to hide them when he wasn't carrying. He had a place in mind for that.

He finished the drink, switched off the lights and opened the blinds; and sat on the couch looking out across the midnight lights of Chicago. He was favorably impressed by the city; but this was where he'd perform the duties of his mission of retribution.

Spalter had met him at O'Hare Airport Saturday morning. There'd been the desultory commonplaces of introductions and small talk: "I think you're going to like it here." Spalter had checked him into the Continental Plaza and then, even though it was Saturday, had taken him by taxi down into the Loop to show him the downtown district and the office where Paul would work. It was Paul's first contact with the strident self-consciousness of Chicago and it had been several days before he'd understood that Spalter was not unusual: neither a Chamber of Commerce crank nor a conventioneering loudmouth. Chicago's boosterism was built-in standard equipment. When they realized you were from out of town they launched into their rehearsed litanies: this was the tallest building in the world; that was the biggest post office in the world; there was the busiest airport in the world. They were as insistent and oblivious as Texans.

Spalter was a clever administrator in his forties, not more than ten pounds heavier than he'd been at half that age when he'd spent two seasons as a halfback at Northwestern: big and bulky but religious about keeping in shape. His good-natured personality probably concealed a certain amount of cold-blooded pragmatism because it took more than sheer charm to achieve an executive vice-presidency with an accounting firm the size of Childress Associates. There wasn't much doubt he had stabbed a few backs.

Saturday morning Spalter had taken him down State

Street past the shops and department stores through gaudy decorations and thronging pre-Christmas shoppers. The narrow monolithic canyons of the Loop reminded Paul of the Wall Street financial district: nearly every building seemed to be a bank. Traffic crawled under the noisy El tracks.

The office was in a building at 313 Monroe near Wacker in the heart of the Loop. The building might have been designed in the 1920s by an enthusiast who had understood more history than architecture: its façade was a tribute to at least three classic styles. The ninth-floor offices were deserted for the weekend but Spalter had shown him dutifully from the boardroom and the chairman's corner suite through computer rooms and mailroom and Spalter's own sanctum and finally a well-appointed office which already had Paul's name in gilt on the door.

"You'll like it, Paul. We're go-getters here—it's our inferiority complex. We're competing with the New York hotshots and we know we've got to be ahead of them just to stay even. Keeps us on our toes, let me tell you."

Spalter had signed them out under the eye of the lobby guard and walked Paul down Monroe to the University Club. It reminded Paul of the Harvard Club in New York: primly old-fashioned with forced humorless masculinity.

Spalter chose a pair of armchairs and ordered drinks. "We were doing some audit work for a plastics plant on the South Side. They had an unannounced sit-down strike and the manager out there didn't know what the hell to do— he had a rush order to bring in on a penalty contract. He and Childress were having lunch in the club here and the plant manager was moaning about the strike. Our esteemed chairman of the board proved what executive genius is all about, that day."

"How?"

"Childress told the manager what to do. The manager walked into the factory and told the strikers as long as they were on a sit-in they might as well make themselves comfortable. He brought in bourbon and beer by the case. When the strikers were pretty well stewed he sent in a busload of professional ladies to entertain them. They were having the time of their lives in there, and then the manager brought the men's wives in to see what was going on. Well the strike was called off in less than an hour."

Paul joined his laughter and Spalter sat back and covered his evident hesitation by turning his drink to catch the light, examining it. Paul said, "I'm looking forward to it—working for a firm with a sense of humor."

"There's enough laughs, most of the time. Childress is a born practical joker though—you want to watch out for a while until you catch onto his style. It's nothing crude—he won't put exploding cigars in your desk humidor, nothing like that. He saves the nasty pranks for people on his hate list. The manager of our building gave us some trouble a couple of years ago and Childress got beautiful revenge. You know all those bulk-rate catalogues and magazine subscription blurbs, the stuff you're overwhelmed with when you get on mailing lists? Well Childress filled out dozens of the damn things in the name of the building manager. The poor guy was buried in magazines and mail-order junk he hadn't ordered. I think he almost went to court on two or three of them. Took him months to get it sorted out—he was a complete wreck."

Paul had met John V. Childress only once, when the chairman was visiting New York. Ives, the senior partner of Paul's firm of CPA's in New York, had been very understanding about Paul's need to get away. Ives had introduced Paul to John Childress and used his influence to obtain the Chicago position for Paul. In his brusque way Ives was the kindest of men; Paul was immodest enough to know he'd been valuable to the firm and Ives hadn't wanted to lose him. But Paul had been insistent. Esther's death had overwhelmed him, the reminders in New York were too much for him: he had to make a fresh start in new surroundings. When Carol had died it had been the final straw.

Spalter sipped his scotch. "It's not always fun and games working for Childress. He works our asses off."

"That's the way I like it."

"I've heard that about you. I think you're going to fit in just fine, Paul—and what's more important to you, I think we're going to fit in just fine with you."

Spalter was a bit of a bullshit artist but Paul rather liked him. He made a gesture with his drink.

"Christmas coming up fast," Spalter said. "We won't really be getting back into gear until after the first of the year. Childress and I both think it might be a good idea if you spent your first couple of weeks just relaxing, getting to know Chicago a bit before you plunge into the office routine. After the holidays there'll be a pile-up of income-tax work and you may not have too much time for familiarization. Anyhow, take the holidays off, find yourself a house, get settled in, get to know our town a bit. There'll probably be several Christmas and New Year's parties— I'll keep you posted. You can report in to work on Monday the sixth. How's that sound?"

It gave him more than two weeks; he agreed to it with suitable gratitude.

Spalter sat forward, elbows on knees. "Stop me if I'm out of line. But naturally we've heard a little about why you decided to move here. Do you mind talking about it?"

"Not any more. But why go into it?"

"The place is full of rumors. I think you can understand that. It'd be a good idea if we could put a lid on the gossip before people start looking at you as if you've got two heads."

"What gossip?"

"For instance they're saying you went to pieces."

Paul managed to smile.

"You don't look to me like a man who's gone to pieces."

"It's a dreary story. All too commonplace."

"Your wife was mugged, I gather."

"My wife and my daughter. They were attacked in our apartment. My wife died in the hospital. My daughter died two months later."

"As a result of the attack?"

"Indirectly." He didn't elaborate. Carol had been institutionalized: catatonic withdrawal. In her mind she had fled from recollections too horrible to face. She'd become a vegetable. He'd watched her retreat: the steady terrible escape from reality until she'd collapsed into the final trance, unable to talk or see or hear or feed herself. Death had been, perhaps, an accident: she had choked on her own tongue and had been dead nearly half an hour before the nurse discovered it.

"Did they apprehend the muggers?"

"No."

"Christ."

Paul drained his glass and set it down gently. "Esther and Carol didn't have any money with them, you see. Three or four dollars, that was all. The muggers got mad at them because they didn't have money."

"Jesus."

Paul met his eyes. "They gave them terrible beatings."

Spalter looked away. "I'm—"

"No. Maybe I'm the one who should apologize. I told it to you that way for a reason."

"To prove that you can face it—that you haven't gone around the bend."

"That's right. There are things you have no control over. To me it's as if they were both killed by an earthquake or an unexpected cancer. It's in the past. I've got my grief but we've all got sorrows to live with. Either we carry on or we throw in the towel. I'm not the suicide type. Do you go to the movies?"

"Now and then," Spalter said indifferently.

"I'm a Western nut. The rituals are relaxing, I find. In every other Western there's a line—'You play the cards you're dealt.' "

"And that's what you're doing."

"There's really not much choice," Paul lied.

Spalter brooded into his empty glass. The waiter brought fresh drinks and Spalter signed the chit. "My daughter's boy friend lives on Howard Street. I guess you wouldn't know the area. Anyway a few months ago the city in its wisdom put up no-parking signs there, and Chet had to find overnight parking on the side streets after that. Within a month his car had been stripped twice. Recently the council passed an ordinance to repeal the no-parking restrictions out there, but what the hell kind of solution to a problem is that? I suppose our troubles won't come as any surprise to *you* but I'd be kidding if I said we didn't have a hell of a crime problem in Chicago. A thousand murders —most of them never solved. It's no promised land."

Paul didn't want to be drawn into speculations about the Crime Problem. The best way to avoid being betrayed by a slip of the tongue was to say nothing at all.

Spalter talked on. He darted from topic to topic and sometimes there were no discernible connectives. He wasn't a stream-of-consciousness talker; he was being dutifully— and good-naturedly—helpful, telling Paul things he thought a newcomer ought to know. Paul was grateful when the subject moved away from crime.

He tried to put some show of interest on his face; he was finding it hard to keep his attention on Spalter's pointers about the firm's internal politics. There was useful data in Spalter's anecdotes about office feuds and jealousies, his throwaway character sketches, his quick run-down on the companies for which Childress Associates regularly did audits. It would be important for Paul to familiarize himself with these oddments. He intended to do good work at Childress: he'd always taken pride in his abilities but now there was something else—he couldn't risk drawing attention to himself by displaying any sudden deterioration in the professional capabilities for which he was known. It would require more effort than before because the job was no longer the center of his life; now it was merely a source of income and a camouflage for the appeasement of his private demons.

After lunch they had left the club and Spalter, burly in his topcoat, had ridden with Paul as far as the hotel. Paul had declined Spalter's dinner invitation, pleading tiredness after his flight. When Spalter was gone he had crossed the street and prowled the arcade of the John Hancock complex until he found a magazine shop where he bought Chicago maps and guidebooks and all three local newspapers and a *New York Times* which had a page 40 column about the police department's continuing unsuccessful search for the vigilante who had used the same revolver, according to ballistics reports, to kill seventeen people in the streets of New York over a five-week span. Of the seventeen victims of his retributive vengeance, fourteen had criminal records and two others had been found dead with stolen property on or near their bodies. It was possible he had saved a score of innocent lives.

In his hotel room he had found a printed card from the management:

We urge your use of the Safety Deposit Vaults available at no charge at the Front Office. Please DO NOT *leave furs, jewelry, cameras, money or* ANY VALUABLES *in your room. Illinois State laws relieve the hotel from liability for loss, excepting when valuables have been properly placed in a safety deposit vault. . . . Please use the* DOUBLE LOCKS *on your guest room door. We wish you a most enjoyable stay.*

That night he'd slept with his wallet inside his pillowcase.

Ω
_____

4

¶ CHICAGO, DEC. 17TH—The bodies of two men, shot to death, were found early this morning on the sidewalk in the 2000 block on North Mohawk.

Discovery of the homicide victims was reported to the police by Philip Frank, 43, a passing motorist.

A police spokesman identified the dead men as Edward A. Smith, 23, of 1901 Washtenaw, and Leroy Thompson, 22, address uncertain. According to the police, both men had criminal records for assault and robbery; Thompson was serving a suspended two-year sentence at the time of his death.

The shattered remains of an empty wine bottle were found near the bodies. A police spokesman said one of the dead men, Smith, was found with a knife lying near his hand.

Both victims were shot twice. Police report that ballistics investigation suggests the same .38 revolver was used to fire all four bullets. "But we're not absolutely certain," the police spokesman cautioned. "The bullets recovered from the bodies are badly misshapen and fragmented. They're almost certainly hollow-point bullets, and we're going to need further laboratory examination before we can be positive they all came from the same weapon."

No motive has been put forth for the homicides. District detectives are investigating.

The two homicides raise this year's number of gunshot deaths within Chicago's city limits to 856.

Ω
5

AT THE BAR, men ruminated secretively over their beer, looking up at newcomers and looking away again. Toward the back a group of hearty men shouted across one another. The room had dark wood, poor light and a lingering aura of tobacco smoke and grain whiskey. Specks of dust twirled under the lights.

Paul found a space at the bar. "I'll have a beer."

The bartender named half a dozen brands; Paul picked one. While he waited for it he studied the crowd and decided the noisy group at the back contained his men.

The bar was a block from the Tribune Tower and equidistant from the *Daily News* and *Sun-Times* pressrooms. Paul had chosen it because it was likely to be the informal headquarters of the city's news reporters and he suspected it might be the best source of information about the unfamiliar city. He needed to know about Chicago: he needed to know how the city worked, where its stresses were, how the police operated.

He carried his beer toward the back and hovered at the edge of the loud group. There were nine or ten men and women roughed up by alcohol and cigarettes and the cynicisms of insiders' experience. It was only half past six but they'd been at their drinks long enough to be doing more talking than listening: insistent assertions roared cacophonously back and forth. They were talking about the mayor and the machine but he couldn't sort out much at all in the babble.

At the edge of it two men observed without participating and Paul maneuvered himself closer to them. One stood against the bar, wincing at the racket; the other was a moon-faced bald man with a drink in his hand. "Don't flatter yourself, Mike. You didn't invent the hangover."

"The hell. I'm going to take out a patent on this one." Mike waved angrily at the oblivious bartender.

The bald man said, "When he comes I advise you to make it a double. This joint serves thimble-size shots."

Paul was between Mike and the bartender; he turned and managed to attract the bartender's eye. The bartender came along the slot: "Yes sir?"

Paul gestured to the man behind him. "This gentleman wants a drink."

Mike turned, reached an arm past Paul's shoulder and slapped his palm on the bar. "Double Dewar's straight up."

The bald man said, "Wish I could afford that."

"Try not to get fired so often then." Mike smiled through bad teeth at Paul. "My friend, you've just saved a life. Name's Ludlow, there, buddy. Mike Ludlow."

"Fred Mills," Paul lied. "Nice to meet you."

"A new face," said the bald man. "Christ you must have wandered into this crazy farm by mistake, Mr. Mills. My

name's Dan O'Hara. Don't believe a word this man tells you
—he's a no-good drunk."

Ludlow reached for his drink when the bartender set it
before him: he raised it carefully to his lips. "Not a drunk,
O'Hara. An alcoholic. You've got no subtlety, you stupid
mick, you don't understand vital distinctions."

"He's a drunk," O'Hara confided. "Don't listen to him."

Ludlow swallowed most of the drink and closed his eyes.
"Listen. Shoot their mouths off all night long until the beer
runs out and nobody listens to a word of it." Paul had to
lean forward to catch his words; the crowd's racket was
intense.

The bartender put a bill on the bar in front of Ludlow
and Paul picked it up, doing it quietly but knowing O'Hara
saw it. Paul turned it face down and put a five-dollar bill
on it and waited for the change.

O'Hara had a mild brogue. "All right, Mr. Mills, what
can we do for you?" He said it amiably but he'd made the
connection immediately.

"I'm from New York, my company transferred me out
here. I don't know a damn thing about Chicago."

"And you've come to the fountainhead. Smart lad."

Ludlow drained his glass and put it down. "I'll buy the
next round. Thanks for the drink, sport. What line are you
in?"

"Security systems." Paul had it pat on his tongue. "Burglar
alarms for the home, electronic security—everything in the
gadget line. We're a new company, just breaking into the
Midwest market."

"And you want to get to know your new turf." O'Hara
put his beer glass down beside Ludlow's. "I'll tell you what,
Mike, why don't we take Mr. Mills around the corner where
we can hear ourselves think. Can't give the man serious ad-
vice in this heathen bedlam."

Paul gathered his change and left a tip on the bar. Ludlow gave him a friendly touch on the shoulder and steered him toward the door in O'Hara's broad wake.

A few snowflakes undulated into Rush Street but it was nothing that would settle; the pavements were hardly moist. O'Hara turned up the sheepskin collar of his bulky cloth coat. "Another bleedin' slush Christmas, I predict."

"Always bitching about the rain." Ludlow had a harsh laugh. "This bastard was *born* in a country where it rains twenty-four hours a day."

They turned a corner and went under the El tracks into a sandwich parlor with chrome-and-formica booths; the lighting was bright but there was a bar along the near wall and the place was nearly empty. Paul sat on a stool and found himself bracketed between O'Hara and Ludlow. O'Hara had inky fingernails: he held up a hand and beckoned the barmaid. "Dewar's straight up, darlin', and a Miller's for my cheap friend. What's for you, Mr. Mills?"

"Beer's fine."

Ludlow put his money on the bar. "Well now, where do we start?"

O'Hara coughed. "Let's find out what it is our friend wants to know."

"We know what he wants to know. He wants to know what kind of place Chicago is."

"I'll answer that in a sentence. When derelicts go slumming, they go to Chicago."

Ludlow said, "O'Hara don't know what the hell he's talking about. He writes think-pieces, he's a political reporter. Every six months they fire him because somebody from the Cook County machine leans on his editor. Me, I stay on the news beat, I've been a crime reporter eight years in this town. I'm the one you want to pump. Forget this ignorant mick."

"Watch it now, Mike."

"I'll give you some facts," Ludlow said, more to O'Hara than to Paul. "Fact, O'Hara. There's a robbery in this town every three minutes around the clock. Fact, we had eight hundred homicides last year and we're way above that record this year. Crime's up fifteen per cent overall. Fact, O'Hara —less than one per cent of Chicago's crimes are solved, in the sense that some joker gets tried and convicted and sent to the slammer."

O'Hara drank and spoke in a voice made breathless by the beer. "Statistics."

"Here's a statistic, Mr. Mills. An infant boy born in Chicago today has a better chance of being murdered than an American soldier in World War Two had to get killed in combat. If the crime rate keeps increasing the way it's going now, one Chicagoan in every fifteen will be a homicide victim. Dead, dead."

"Crime rate." O'Hara made a sound: it might have been a sneeze. "Listen to this fool." He turned and poked Paul's sleeve. "I'll give you real facts. We're living in an occupied war zone. The city's chopping and slashing itself to ruin. It's what the ecologists call a behavioral sink. An intolerable overcrowding that leads to the inevitable collective massacre." He pronounced the polysyllables with exaggerated precision.

"Yeah," Ludlow said obscurely. "Yeah, yeah."

"Chicago," O'Hara said in a mock-wistful voice. "It's watching the lake shore and waiting for some scaly grade-B monster to loom out of the sludge and step on the whole thing—the buildings and the people and the rats that bite the people. And in the meantime the cops go right on vagging prostitutes and shaking down storekeepers while a sniper picks off four drivers on the John F. Kennedy Expressway."

31

"Twenty-six homicides last weekend," Ludlow said. There was no perceptible emotion in his voice. "Sixty hours, twenty-six murders."

Paul said, "Why?"

"Why what?"

"It shouldn't be like that," Paul said. "People shouldn't have to be afraid."

Ludlow only laughed off-key.

O'Hara said, "Listen, I talked to a guy in Cicero—he's eighty years old and he's grateful because it was only the third time his apartment got knocked over."

"Why does everybody put up with it?"

"We're all sheep," O'Hara said. "Sure. Last weekend there was a mugger working the Christmas shoppers down in the Loop. Wearing drag, but it was a guy. Transvestite. He got pissed because a dame refused to hand over her handbag. The guy in drag shot the woman to death in broad daylight right in front of the bus terminal on Randolph."

"Sweet Jesus." Paul had the glass in his hand; suddenly it felt cold.

Ludlow sang sotto voce: "Chicago, Chicago, it's my kind of town," confusing two songs, possibly deliberately.

Paul said, "The mugger in women's clothes—was he caught?"

"That one they caught," O'Hara said. "Of course for every one they nail, there's a hundred they don't."

"You'll do a fantastic business in this town," Ludlow told Paul. "Not that it'll do any good."

"Why?"

"The police won't answer the alarms half the time."

"Apathy," O'Hara said. "Two guys got hit last night over on Mohawk. Thirty-eight revolver, four shots fired right on a residential street. Nobody phoned in a report. Everybody who lives on that block must have heard the shots. But it had to wait for some guy driving by to spot the corpses and report it to the cops, and they took their time getting there."

"You try to walk in this town, you hear footsteps behind you it's like the sound of grenades. A walk in Chicago after dark is a combat mission."

"It's politics, bloody politics."

"Listen to him. Everything's politics to the mick."

"There was a time when the Cook County machine was good for something. You got ripped off, the clubhouse would provide a meal and even a job for you, and a lawyer for the guy who ripped you off. It was all part of the community in those days. Now it's a political battlefield. The big shots have drawn back, there's just no contact at all between the politicians and the communities. The machine answers criticism by closing ranks—there are no lines of communication any more. The cops are on the take or they're not on the take, but either way there's no old-fashioned dedication there any more. It's just a job to those guys—you put as little as you can into it, you take as much as you can out of it. If they start busting heads they're accused of police brutality and if they don't bust heads they're accused of corruption—you can't blame them. The judicial system's fucked up beyond belief because nobody knows how to treat crime any more. You kill somebody on the street, you cop a plea, the judge lets you off with jail time served and a year's probation. The rewards for crime keep increasing while the cost of committing crime keeps decreasing. The chances are you won't get caught, and if you get caught the chances are you won't get tried, and if you get tried the chances are you won't get convicted, and if you get convicted the chances are you won't go to prison. The crooks have got odds of a thousand to one in their favor. The rest of us are torn between retribution and compassion—we don't know what we ought to do, so we don't do anything at all."

"The people know zip about crime," Ludlow said.

O'Hara said, "Let's have another drink. Mr. Mills is buying."

Ω

6

BEFORE HE LEFT THEM the two journalists had consumed prodigiously and their bickering had lost its amicability: they were threatening each other like blowhards in a Western saloon. The bartender intervened but it only persuaded O'Hara and Ludlow to take the quarrel outside into the night where they started feinting like boxers in the drifting snow.

Paul faded into the darkness. He had never understood men who fought for fun.

He had nursed two beers for hours and come away with valuable items of information and innuendo. He knew something of the organization and disposition of the police—their districts and patterns of patrol, their levels of diligence and indifference. He had gained a rudimentary idea of the organization of the force's homicide detectives and captains —it was somewhat different from the vertical structure of the New York department—and he'd learned something about the Chicago Crime Commission. He's been told demo-graphic and commercial facts that didn't appear on his street maps—Old Town, New Town, the Lithuanian and Polish and Italian and Chinese neighborhoods, the hard-core centers of the four police districts in which nearly half of Chicago's violent crimes were reported. He'd learned that police surveillance was highest and most efficient in the First Ward—because it was the home ward of the city's venerable political machine and because it included the showcase Loop —and that it was thinnest in the west and southwest districts.

He'd learned a great many details, some of which might prove inaccurate; nevertheless it had been worthwhile and the two reporters had played nicely into his hands. They'd had to: ask a man to talk about a topic on which he con-siders himself an expert and he will happily oblige.

He found his way back along Rush Street to the open lot where his car was parked. He ransomed it, declined a receipt and drove south toward the inferior regions of the city.

He was hunting again. At first in New York he'd tried to rationalize it. He'd walk down Riverside Park late at night with his hand on the gun in his coat pocket, and he'd con-vince himself he was only doing what any peace-loving citizen had a right to do—walk unafraid in a public park. Any predator who might attack him was asking for whatever happened: *It's not my doing, he can leave me alone if he wants to.* But he couldn't delude himself forever. He wasn't strolling in those parks at two o'clock in the morning for exercise or enjoyment. He was prowling for a kill and any other description of it had to be rationalization. The gun in his pocket wasn't there for self-protection. He wasn't defending himself, he was attacking: setting a trap, using himself as the bait and closing the trap when the predator entered it.

He'd asked himself why. He took no pleasure from watching a man die. There was no perverted thrill in it. Inevitably his reaction afterward was painful nausea. He did not feel particularly cleansed or particularly triumphant. Relief, sometimes, that he had come through again without injury; but it wasn't a challenge that thrilled him, it wasn't anything he had to prove to himself—it wasn't macho. He'd spent months thinking of nothing else but there were some things you could analyze to death without ever being able to explain them. It was—what? A sense of obligation? Not a compulsion, not a perverse addiction, no; it wasn't something he felt compelled to do. It was simply something that *ought* to be done. A job, a duty uncertainly defined; he couldn't get closer than that.

When he was deep inside the urban ferment of the South Side ghetto he chose a boulevard lined with shabby stores and drove slowly through the sparse traffic until he saw an open pawn shop. He cruised past it, made the next right turn and had no difficulty finding a place to park; it was not a neighborhood in which you parked your car overnight on the street with any expectation of finding it intact in the morning.

He locked the car carefully and made sure all the windows were shut tight. When he walked back toward the light at the intersection he passed a tall black-bearded man in a wide-brimmed leather hat who moved to the far side of the sidewalk and didn't look at Paul as they passed each other; the tall man receded into the shadows and Paul turned the corner.

There was a thin stream of pedestrian traffic to and from the late-closing supermarket; he went past it, the price placards in the windows and the closed-circuit security eyes high on the walls and the armed private guard near the door. Next to it was a liquor store, closed, a steel grillwork locked over its windows; then an Army-Navy surplus store and finally at the corner the pawnshop overhung by its spherical brass triad. Paul went inside and browsed for five minutes, exchanged not more than four words with the proprietor and returned to the street.

When he reached the sidewalk he had his wallet in his hand and he was counting the money in it as if he had just put it there. He thrust the wallet clumsily into his outside coat pocket, making a show of it, and walked back past the supermarket to the next corner, moving his hand inside the coat pocket, switching his grip from the wallet to the .38 revolver.

A policeman, even a dedicated one, had to wait for a crime to be committed within reach before he could act on it. His very presence, in uniform, would discourage the crime's commission in any case. Long ago Paul had learned not to waste his time in fruitless search for felons in the act of committing crimes; the odds were too long. A robbery took place in the city every three minutes according to Mike Ludlow but it was an enormous city and there were three million potential victims.

It was much more certain if you invited them to make you their victim.

When he turned the corner he half-expected to be followed but he wasn't. No one had been tempted by the bulging wallet or the pawnshop customer's evident carelessness.

Dry run: a dud. Well you couldn't expect them to tumble every time.

He continued into the deeper shadows and his eyes had to accustom themselves to the inferior light farther along the block; he turned once, squinting, to make sure no one was tailing him. The sidewalk remained empty. Summoning patience he put his back to the boulevard, relaxed his grip on the gun and continued along the cracked concrete without hurry. As his eyes dilated he looked up along the sagging weathered stoops of the tenements: here and there a dim bulb but most of the entrances were unlit. There was no one in sight: it wasn't a place where you would sit on the porch to take the air. In any case flakes drifted by and the night was too chill for it.

It was only the suggestion of a stirring in the corner of his vision but it made sweat burst out on his palms. He stopped bolt-still.

There by the car. His car.

Nothing.

But when he passed his eyes over the car again he saw a subtle line that wasn't part of the car's silhouette: just visible, a flat shadow no bigger than a paperback book. . . .

He walked forward. Twenty-five feet, twenty and he had it then: it was the flat crown of a hat behind the fender. The man was crouching behind the car and didn't realize quite how high his hat was.

Paul kept walking as if to go by the car. A sidewise glance: the hat was moving, the man was circling behind the car, crabbing his way into the street in order to stay behind cover as Paul walked past.

By the front bumper Paul pivoted on his right foot and leaped between the cars and hauled the Centennial from his pocket. He wheeled past the car and the man looked up in naked amazement—reared back in fear, lost his balance and had to whip one stiff arm behind him to brace his palm against the pavement.

Something extended from the man's hand. The man lifted it as if it were a weapon.

Paul shot him in the face. The man's elbow unlocked and he went down on his back. His leather hat rolled into the center of the street.

The tool rested in his splayed hand: a twisted length of

39

coat-hanger wire. Standard for breaking into car windows.

Paul plugged his key into the door, dived into the car and started it with a gnashing grind. He locked the wheel to the left and cramped the car out of the parking space. He felt it when the rear wheel rolled over the dead man's outstretched arm.

He went down the street without lights: if there was a witness he didn't want his license plate to show. He turned two successive corners before he switched on the headlamps and slipped into the stream of boulevard traffic. He drove up Lake Shore Drive obsessed by the knowledge that he might have left a clue: the print of his rear tire on the dead man's flesh.

He worked it out in his head. He drove right past his apartment building and continued into the North Side and turned off there, cruising until he found a quiet block. Ignored by occasional passing cars he jacked up the car and changed the rear tire, putting the spare on the car. Then he unscrewed the valve of the tire and bled the air out of it.

When it had gone soft he used the tire iron to pry the tire off the wheel rim. He didn't have proper tools and it was a hard job; he worked steadily, without desperation but steadied by necessity. Finally the tire came off the wheel and he drove west until he found a weedy lot cluttered with trash. He wiped the tire off, wary of fingerprints, and left it there amid the junk; then he drove back to the apartment. Tomorrow he'd buy a new spare tire.

It was well after midnight by the time he'd cleaned and reloaded the Centennial. He switched on the radio and tuned to the all-news station but there was no report of the South Side killing yet. At one o'clock he turned it off and showered and went to bed, trying to put faces on the images of the three men who always drifted in the back of his mind: the savages who'd broken into the apartment and mauled Esther and Carol.

He'd never found them; he'd never expected to. When you set out to eradicate a disease-bearing species of insects you didn't hunt for particular individual insects.

Ω
_____

7

IT WAS a cool day oppressed by a hydrocarbon haze. Sea gulls from the lake flew inland reconnaissance over the city. It was four o'clock; soon it would be dusk. Paul walked into the shop: *Tax Returns Prepared—CHECKS CASHED—Xerox While-U-Wait.* He went to the check-cashing counter and engaged in twenty seconds' conversation with the cashier: he asked direction to the nearest El station, the location of which he knew already but for anyone watching him it established that he'd gone to the check-cashing window. He took his wallet out of his pocket and fiddled with it before he turned away from the window; he was still counting the money in it when he emerged onto the street.

He had performed the ritual several times and it hadn't tempted anyone yet but he kept at it because he needed at least one more immediate target to convince the press of his existence.

When he reached the street a police cruiser was prowling by with its roof-bar of siren and lights and its lettered decals on the door. Paul counted his money again and then put the wallet in his coat pocket and turned the corner into a street lined with old frame houses streaked with watermarks.

Halfway down the block he stopped and patted his pockets as if he'd lost something. It gave him an excuse to turn a circle on his heels and search the sidewalk behind him. Down at the corner a thin jittery figure in a threadbare jacket stood restlessly: a youth bouncing on his arches like an athlete waiting to compete. Behind him a woman went across the street jerking a small wailing child by the hand.

A second youth appeared and joined the first.

Paul reached down and picked up an invisible object and put it in his pocket and walked on.

To his right a windowless clapboard wall had been decorated with spray-gun artwork. The houses beyond were dreary and lifeless. Chicago's slums were spacious and airy by comparison with New York's crowded high tenement buildings; the streets were wide, the buildings low. But the desolation had the same smell.

He kept the wallet in the same pocket as the gun for two reasons. If a mugger demanded his wallet he could produce the gun instead. But if a policeman went into that pocket Paul wanted him to find the $250 cash in the wallet.

The two kids watched him from the corner behind him: he saw their reflections in the rear window of a panel truck as he walked by it. They were all jerks and jitters: wired as if they'd been plugged into a wall outlet. Addicts? He had no way of diagnosing; maybe they were only natural mannerisms. But when he reached the end of the block and continued along the second block he had a chance, when looking both ways for traffic before crossing the street, to

43

see the two kids out of the corner of his eye and they were following him at a discreet distance. His hands began to sweat: the familiar telltale.

He slowed the pace imperceptibly. His car was near the end of the block. A block farther along the empty street a traffic light blinked red, on and off. Daylight was draining out of the sky. He tasted the brass of fear on his tongue.

The two kids were running now. He heard them come.

Ω
_____

8

¶ CHICAGO, DEC. 19TH—Two teen-age boys were shot to death on the South Side late yesterday, apparently by the same revolver that has killed three others on Chicago streets in the past 72 hours.

The boys, Ernesto Delgado, 16, and his brother Julio, 15, of 4415 W. 21st Place, were found dead on a Wolcott Avenue sidewalk at 5:10 p.m. yesterday by a passing Chicago police patrol car.

According to a preliminary examination by the police laboratory, the bullets that killed the Delgado brothers may have been fired by the same .38 revolver alleged to have been the weapon used in last night's killing of James Washington, 26, on Lowe Avenue, and in the prior night's homicides on North Mohawk, the victims of which were identified as Edward A. Smith, 23, and Leroy Thompson, 22.

Police Captain Victor Mastro this morning said, "We may have a 'vigilante' on our hands."

Mastro spoke in reference to the recent spate of "vigilante" killings in New York City. They have been discussed widely by the national press and television.

The three adult homicide victims all had criminal records, Mastro said. And while juvenile records cannot be published, a police spokesman remarked that the Delgado brothers were alleged to have been heroin addicts. A neighbor, interviewed this morning, described the two boys as "violent and vicious kids."

Captain Mastro stated that photographs of the bullets in all five cases have been sent to New York for comparison with those found in the bodies of the victims of the alleged "vigilante" killer in that city.

Chicago Police Chief John Colburn, asked to comment, said, "I'd rather not speculate at this point until we've got more facts to work on. At the moment we've assigned detectives to investigate these homicides and the connection, if any, between them. It's too early to jump to conclusions."

A "VIGILANTE" IN CHICAGO?
Commentary
by Michael Ludlow

Reports from the police blotter indicate that a "vigilante"-style executioner may be prowling the streets of Chicago, possibly inspired by the New York killings attributed to that city's unidentified "vigilante."

Whether or not such vigilantes exist, speculation and rumor have fostered a wave of emphasis on the "crime problem" which seems unprecedented even in this age of soaring crime rates and law-and-order politics.

Despite the nation's unemployment, recession, inflation, revelations of political chicanery, crop failures, petroleum and energy crises, and all the other burdens our society has to bear—despite all these tribulations— every poll conducted in the past weeks has indicated emphatically that the "crime crisis" has become the number one concern of Americans, helped along clearly by New York's (and Chicago's?) "vigilante."

It is a concern that is nearly unique, in that it is shared by members of every economic level, race, age group and region.

Obviously it is more than momentary hysteria. It may be true, as has been alleged, that the "vigilante" is a myth created either by New York's police or by the news media; but the fact remains that crime in America has become a true crisis.

We can't pretend it doesn't exist and hope it will go away. Quibbling about the inaccuracies in the FBI's recent Uniform Crime Report statistics will not change the fact that ordinary people are not safe on the streets, or even in their homes. If a citizen is so terrified that he refuses to leave his locked apartment, he has been deprived of his freedom. His civil liberties have been revoked just as surely as have those of the vigilante's presumed victims.

Vigilantism is not an answer. We cannot solve the crime problem by increasing the number of murders.

But we must act.

It is time our institutions fulfilled the missions for which they were established. The inadequacy of police budgets, the alarming back-up of cases on the calendars of overcrowded criminal courts, the overwhelming prevalence of plea-bargaining in felony cases, and the revolving-door bail-bond situation that puts felons back on the streets within hours after their arrest—all these and other aspects of the police-judicial-penal systems are becoming recognized as intolerable weaknesses that threaten the very survival of our democracy's structure of freedom and law.

Legal punishment, to deter, must be immediate and impartial. The only thing known to deter criminal acts is the reasonable certainty that they will be exposed and that prosecution, conviction and punishment will follow. Without that reasonable certainty we risk the rise of chaotic anarchy in the form of vigilantism—the citizenry taking the law into its own hands, mindlessly and individually. The "vigilante" is ample evidence that our institutions must act now—before it is too late.

Ω

9

FRIDAY EVENING it began to rain. Reflected neon colors melted and ran along the wet streets. Paul sat in his parked car and switched on the radio softly to have company. Under an awning a man with a square dark beard dressed in black coat and wide black hat was reading a newspaper, turning the pages left to right. Girls in shabby clothes paraded the boulevard under two-dollar umbrellas with a pretended indifference to the eyes that followed them; smudges of dirty illumination drifted across the bellies of the clouds.

Old Town: night life, drunks, tourists, night-blooming girls. Someone came out of a cocktail lounge near the car and a gust of hard rock music blew across the pavement, loud enough to reach Paul's ears despite his closed car windows and the muttering radio. There was a busy singles' club and next door to it a spiritual adviser (Palms Read). The bearded Jew licked his thumb and turned a page of his newspaper. Raindrops glistened, caught in his beard.

Two youths stopped to gaze at the photos under the marquee of a "Topless-Live-Girls" emporium across the street; the youths moved on into the rain, a bit marble-eyed or perhaps it was only the way the lights reflected from their eyes. At the corner they stopped under a hooded whip-lamp on a silvered stalk; their clothes were pasted against them and they must have had rain inside their shoes but they didn't seem to mind. They talked and one of them shrugged and then they moved on.

Paul was watching the drunks emerge from the clubs because those were the obvious marks. He'd seen two couples stagger out of the singles' club but they'd got into a car parked directly across the street. A drunk had come out of the topless joint but he'd been collected by a taxi which evidently had been summoned by phone.

There was a counter food place on the near corner and he could almost smell the vapors of the frying fat; people drifted in and out of the place but one group had taken possession of part of the counter shortly after Paul arrived and they were still there: toughs, the night crazies. He could see them through the smoke-stained plate glass. They'd have been loitering on the street but for the rain. They wore the uniforms of their kind—leather, tight trousers, boots with high heels, the hats tipped far to one side.

After a while one man separated himself from that group and moved into the doorway to look up and down at the street. His face seemed to be covered with sores or the pits of some old disease.

A couple had left the hard rock club. The man with the pitted face watched them unfurl their umbrella and hurry away. Paul watched all of them, his attention returning time after time to the man in the doorway. But the tough didn't move, not even when a tall heavy black man approached the place and had to squeeze past him to get inside.

The old Jew turned another page. Paul wondered what he was waiting for. A friend?

The man with the pitted face stepped out of the doorway after a long time. He crossed to stand under the marquee of the topless club, his hat obscuring the "Go-Go" lettering beside the doors. He lit a cigarette. The light was very low; the cigarette described a red arc in the dimness as it came away from his lips and dimmed.

Paul felt the stir of his blood. He had become sensitive to the subtle recognition signs of the predators. He'd heard it said that in Africa a herd of game antelope might allow a lion to prowl very close by without taking alarm because somehow they could sense whether or not the lion was hungry and if it wasn't hungry it was not to be regarded as a threat. Paul might have passed the man with the pitted face and not given him a thought at another time; but tonight the man was hungry and Paul knew it.

He'd known it the other night—the two men on the stoop near the Irish bar: he'd known they'd come after him.

He knew it the same way with this one. He turned, deciding which bar to go into: he'd follow the same drill, do the drunk act, draw the man with the pitted face after him.

He settled on the singles' bar and got out of the car, locking it behind him, crossing the sidewalk quickly and pausing under the shelter of the awning. He glanced across the street, but the man wasn't watching him—the man's whole attention was fixed on a woman walking wearily past him under an umbrella: a middle-aged woman with a handbag carelessly pendulant from her crooked elbow. Reasonably expensive clothes: a businesswoman perhaps. There were enclaves of fashionable housing in the neighborhood: perhaps she was on her way home after a long day's work keeping the shop open in the Christmas rush.

She wasn't drunk but she dragged her feet, very tired; she

turned the corner and went out of sight into a side street and that was when the man with the pitted face made his move. The cigarette dropped into a puddle and the man walked swiftly toward the corner.

Paul turned his collar up against the rain and went across the street, sprinting to dodge a passing car, jumping up on the curb fast enough to avoid being splashed by the tires of the next one.

The man with the pitted face had followed the woman around the corner. Paul approached the corner quickly, pushing both hands into his coat pockets, and made the turn as if it were his own neighborhood and he knew the way home.

The woman was a half block distant. An elderly man approached her.

Paul stopped briefly: there was no sign of the man with the pitted face.

He heard the elderly man speak to the woman with the dignified courtesy of inebriation: "Would you like a drink, madam?"

The woman shook her head and walked past him; the man smiled wistfully and continued toward Paul.

Paul went by him, moving more quickly in the woman's wake: he was looking for the shadow which shouldn't be there.

He overtook the woman. No sign of another presence anywhere; had the elderly drunk scared the predator away?

He went past the slow-moving woman and strode on, nearly a block. Here it was quite dark: the street light at the corner had burned out. It was an unusually narrow street and it had a bad feel.

Paul went up a six-step flight into the covered entrance of a house. He stopped there in complete darkness and turned to look back.

The woman approached with the stolid stride of weariness, umbrella-stem resting on her shoulder; the handbag dangled from her elbow, flopping against her coat.

An entranceway behind her: an apparitious shape appeared.

The man with the pitted face.

He was behind the woman and she wasn't aware of him. Paul saw him draw a knife from his pocket. The man shot the blade silently—not a switchblade; it was a gravity-action knife. He loomed behind the woman.

Paul braced his arms against the wall, taking aim. He could hardly see the sights. It wasn't much more than thirty feet but he didn't want to risk hitting the woman and he withheld his fire, waiting a clear target.

The man with the pitted face reached from behind, gripped the handbag in his free hand and brought the knife up. It sliced cleanly through the strap and he carried the handbag away in his left hand.

The woman froze in alarm; she was turning, backing away in terror. Paul had his clear shot now and he steadied his aim.

The old Jew materialized from nowhere: suddenly he was right behind the man with the handbag.

Paul held his fire. The chilly sweat of fear streamed down his ribs.

The Jew had a gun.

"Turn around and hit the wall."

The man with the handbag gaped at him.

"*Move.*" The Jew shoved him hard. "Police officer. You're under arrest." The Jew's voice was young, strong.

Paul saw him kick the man's feet apart and force him against the wall in the frisk position. "Ma'am, you all right?"

"I—yes, yes I'm fine. . . ."

53

The Jew patted the man for weapons and Paul saw him bring out the handcuffs.

Paul pushed the Centennial back into his pocket.

The woman began to speak: a stream of words spilling over with relief and gratitude. The Jew prodded the man with the pitted face; the three of them moved away toward the lights of the intersection, the woman clutching her handbag.

Finally they were gone but Paul stood rooted above the steps, terrified by the memory of his paralysis. When the Jew had appeared it had taken him by surprise and he had been frozen by an alarm so abrupt it had prevented any thought of flight.

It wasn't the fear that disturbed him. Fear was natural. It was the loss of control. Taken by surprise, his domination of the situation destroyed, he had been powerless for that moment despite the gun in his hand.

He went down the steps. It was something he had to sort out: he knew he was all right so long as he had control of events but he hadn't realized how badly he could be shaken by the unexpected.

He'd have to find a way to conquer that. Either that or make sure he was never taken by surprise again.

Ω

10

¶ CHICAGO, DEC. 21ST—An Old Town police stakeout paid off last night when Joseph Crubb was arrested while allegedly in the act of snatching a woman's purse on Oldham Place.

Police described the arrest as the "first break" in their campaign, begun four days ago, to "corral the gang of thugs who've been ripping off the Old Town area."

A spokesman for the district squad said, "The stakeouts will continue until we've broken up the entire gang."

Suspect Crubb, 23, of 2473 W. 96th Street, will be arraigned in Criminal Court Monday morning.

Ω
_____

11

THE NEIGHBORHOOD looked like a place where children grew up quickly. Anything and everything probably was for sale if you knew where to go and what name to ask for. In its midst, strangely, the Cook County Criminal Courthouse loomed opposite an expanse of vacant land.

Behind the courthouse stood a monolith that looked like photographs he'd seen of San Quentin: high stone wall, machine-gun towers. When he turned the corner he saw the legend carved in stone above it. Cook County Jail.

It had occurred to him there were more efficient ways of finding the predators than stalking dark streets at random. This place, the court, was the start of a natural game trail. It captured some of them but it turned others loose, and those who had been turned loose could be followed from this known starting point.

On California Avenue he found a space and parked. He left his guns in the car because they might have metal detectors inside against attempted breakout capers. He hid the guns well and locked the car.

A window washer's crane loomed above the entrance like a gallows. Paul went beneath it into the pillared portico.

People vs. Crubb—Part III. The calendar was penciled on a cork board by the information booth. Paul studied the map of the building, memorized the route and set out through stone hallways.

The courtroom seemed as unreal and musty as a night-club in the daytime. Motes of dust hung in motionless beams of grey that spread weakly from the high windows and seemed to be absorbed before they reached the floor. There was an insistent banging of steam radiators. A long row of people on the rear bench cowered under the cavernous mass of the courtroom, diminished to midgetry by its cruel proportions: a farmer with a scrawny grey neck; a bewildered black woman; a stubborn stubbled man in windbreaker and soft cap; a tall black man, unbreakably aloof; a narrow-faced codger with clever restless eyes; a pudgy youth with his attention fixed on his hands in his lap; a gross woman talking in an insistent whisper to the potbellied little man beside her; two teen-age youths, Latins, with slicked hair and apathetic eyes; a grizzled black overwhelmed by hope-lessness.

Lawyers sprawled in the hard pews, foolscaps spread out on the seats beside them; two or three in the front pews were twisted around in conversation with colleagues behind them. There was a conference of dark-suited men in the far corner beyond the unoccupied bench; one of the men probably was the presiding judge but Paul couldn't single him out and he was almost surprised that there wasn't a man in robes and powdered wig.

The arena below the bench contained two long tables and a solitary lawyer with silver hair had taken possession of one

57

of them; otherwise the arena, like the jury box, was empty.
A queue of five or six lawyers stood patiently at the court
clerk's desk beside the bench, probably ascertaining their
order of appearance in the day's calendar of cases.

Paul chose an inconspicuous pew and sat down behind a
lean angular woman in an orange tweed suit. The sweep of
her eyebrows was emphasized in dark pencil; she had a sleek
tense look. She was talking to a young man in funereal black:
"Frank, it's not good enough. I'm sorry."

"You can't renege on me. I already told him the deal was
made."

"What exactly did you tell him?"

"He cops a manslaughter plea, he gets five and serves
three. Irene, look, the kid's nineteen years old."

"It's not the first time he's been nailed with a knife in
his hand. This time it was covered with the blood of a
seventy-four-year-old woman."

"She didn't die from the stabbing. She had a coronary."

"The coronary was brought on by the assault. Look up
your felony murder law again, Frank. The boy goes up on
first degree, I'm sorry."

"You can't just . . ."

"I told you before, you know. You just didn't listen. You
jumped to conclusions, you assumed . . ."

"What does Pierce say about it?"

"Ask him."

"Maybe I will."

"He always backs up his assistants. He'll throw you out
of the office if you bleat about it."

"What's got you so hot about this one? Would you feel
the same way about this case if the victim had been a man?"

"I won't dignify that with an answer."

"I'll have to file for a continuance. We're not ready to go
to trial."

"Take all the time you want. Nobody wants to railroad him."

"What is it about this kid?"

"He was on my calendar fourteen months ago and I let his lawyer bargain me down to a reduced charge and an SS. The kid went back on the street, and finally he got caught for killing Mrs. Jackquist, but how many others did he stick that knife in before he got caught?"

"You mean you're feeling guilty because you bargained the plea a year ago? For Pete's sake. . . ."

"If I'd gone to trial he'd still be in the slammer right now. Mrs. Jackquist would be alive. Think about that, Frank."

"If every prosecutor felt that way there'd be a waiting line of greybeards on the trial calendar for twenty years."

"Frank, he was pulling the knife out of her when the cop arrested him. There were two witnesses in that hallway who knew the kid personally. There's no chance of eyewitness error. Your client's a vicious animal and he needs putting away. There's nothing more to say."

"I know something about this kid, Irene. His old man . . ."

She spoke very low in precise tones, dropping each word with equal weight like bricks: "I don't give a shit, Frank. I'm sick of people blaming crime on everything but the criminal."

"For Christ's sake, you're acting like you're floating a trial balloon for John Bircher of the year. What's happened to you?"

The woman rocked her hand, fingers splayed; it was the sum of her answer.

The young lawyer snapped his case shut and moved away across the aisle. His rigid back expressed his anger.

Paul leaned forward. "Excuse me, Miss . . ."

Her dark hair swayed when she turned; her alert eyes reserved suspicion. "Yes?"

"I couldn't help overhearing. You're on the district attorney's staff?"

"Yes, but if it's about a case pending before this court I can't . . ."

"It's not. I'm only a spectator."

Her face changed: it made clear her opinion of the morbid curious.

"My name's Paul Benjamin. My wife and daughter were killed by muggers. It makes you take an interest in the criminal justice system."

"I'm very sorry."

"I guess I've spent most of my life like everybody else—badly ignorant of law and crime. I suppose I'm looking for some sort of answers. I'm sorry, I'm not making too much sense. . . ."

She twisted and reached over the back of the bench, offering her hand. "I'm Irene Evans." Her handshake was quick and firm. "When did it happen?"

"Oh it was quite a while ago now, in New York."

"You're just visiting Chicago then?"

"No, I've moved out here. I—couldn't stay there."

"You've picked a strange place to move to. We've got a worse crime problem than New York's."

"You go where the jobs are, I guess."

The judge climbed to the bench; the court stenographer settled behind his machine; lawyers arranged themselves and at the back a prisoner was brought into the room. Irene Evans said, "I have to go to work. Are you free for lunch?"

"I have an appointment. Perhaps tomorrow?"

"Tomorrow's Christmas Eve." She was gathering her papers. "Still, court will be in session. I've got one case to try in the morning. Perhaps if you'd like to meet me here at half past twelve tomorrow. . . ?"

"Thanks very much. I know it's an imposition."

"No. It may give me a chance to think out some questions I've been putting off for too long. You may have done me a favor, you see." She stood up: she wasn't as tall as he'd thought. "Tomorrow lunch, then. I'll look forward to it." She smiled and went toward the rail and he noticed she wore no rings. A lonely woman, he thought.

The defendant and his attorney settled behind a table and Irene Evans took her place at the prosecution's post while one of her fellow assistant DA's crossed to the defense side; there was a murmured conference there and the defense attorney spoke to the judge: "Permission to approach the bench?"

The judge was covering a yawn; he nodded his head and the two attorneys approached and the judge cocked his head to listen to their low voices.

The case was dispatched in moments: an arrangement had been reached, the defense attorney shook his client's hand and returned to the back bench to dismiss his witnesses—the fat woman and the henpecked man. Defendant and officer left the courtroom and another accused entered the room in a policeman's custody. Paul watched the cases parade through the courtroom but his attention drifted; occasionally his attention swiveled to Irene Evans and once from her table she looked at him and smiled a bit.

In the first hour the assembly-line procedure disposed of a half-dozen cases of varying degrees of gravity; he had no doubt that the rubber-stamp system had been preceded by back-room agreements between prosecution and defense; it was clear that the judge's boredom was justified: he gave the court's blessing to each prearranged plea, set sentencing dates in those cases that required them, and called for the next case. Only twice were motions for continuance filed by defense attorneys: cases in which evidently no bargain had been achieved.

Crubb was brought in at 11:45 and when Paul looked back he saw the middle-aged woman whose purse Crubb had snatched; she was sitting with a policeman—the young cop without his old Jew's disguise?—and Paul wondered how long they'd been sitting there; he hadn't noticed their arrival.

An overweight lawyer came out of a front pew and walked back to Crubb; there was a brief whispered conference. Crubb and the lawyer moved forward in the aisle, the lawyer doing most of the talking but Crubb's voice was louder. "Yeah but man what's goin' down now? Sure I know it's bad. Anything that's against the law is bad, ain't it? . . . Man you're a jive-ass, you don't care—what the hell do you care?"

The lawyer talked swiftly and intensely in a voice trained by long practice to reach no farther than his client's ears; Paul couldn't make out a word even though they were sidling past him at arm's length. It was easy enough to guess the gist of the lawyer's monologue. He settled in a front pew with Crubb and kept talking low and fast while the case before the court was decided and then it was Crubb's turn and he went through the gate and paused to look back across the room. His eyes were set very high in his badly pitted face. They were fixed for a moment with arrogant brutality on the middle-aged woman, his victim, the witness; then the lawyer took Crubb's elbow and steered him to the defense table and they stood waiting while the participants of the previous case put their papers together and left the table. Crubb collapsed into his chair and slid down in it until he was sitting on the back of his neck. The lawyer nodded to a man at the prosecution table who came across to him and after a moment the ritual phrase was addressed to the judge: "Arraignment and bail, your honor. Permission to approach the bench?"

The judge nodded.

The whispered tricorn conference at the bench was brief. The judge spoke by rote: "Trial is set for April fourteenth. The prisoner will be released on three hundred dollars bail. Prisoner will approach the bench, please."

It took only a few seconds: the judge warned Crubb of the restrictions of bail and the penalties for jumping it. A bondsman came forward to post the bail. Crubb turned without a word and walked back to the defense table and sat down.

Paul made a show of looking at his watch; he got up then and went toward the door. Irene Evans looked up and he waved to her before he left the room.

He went outside to his car and sat in it. Crubb would turn up any moment, as soon as the papers were signed. Paul reached under the seat for his guns.

Ω
12

THE NUMBER 94 bus had a sickly green two-tone paint job. Paul put the car in drive and followed the bus north on California Avenue into the *barrio*. It reminded him of stretches of the Borough of Queens: commercial shabbiness and nondescript duplex houses. Strong winds buffeted and ripped the racing clouds; the temperature had been dropping all morning and the car radio trumpeted alarums of snow.

Crubb left the bus at Chicago Avenue and walked east on it, shoulders high, boots clicking angrily. Paul waited double-parked and gave him a one-block lead; then he let the car creep forward without feeding any gas. Traffic swished past him in the outside lane.

Friday night Crubb had muffed his hit and come up empty. He'd shown no fear in the courtroom, only a bored arrogance; the hearing and the setting of bail were a slap on the wrist and probably had annoyed and irritated Crubb but certainly they hadn't deterred him. The predator was still hungry.

Crubb entered a pizza café, moving purposefully—he wasn't merely looking for a place to eat. Paul waited in a bus stop. Within a few minutes Crubb reappeared with two companions. They looked like two of the men in the bunch Crubb had been with when Paul had first seen him in Old Town.

The three of them walked, bouncing heel-and-toe, to Western Avenue where they waited for the northbound bus and got aboard it.

He gave the bus several blocks' lead. When it discharged Crubb and his companions he had no trouble recognizing them at the distance; by the time he reached the corner they had walked a block into a neighborhood of small private houses and low brick apartment buildings. Paul glanced at them and drove a block farther along Western, then made the right turn and went two blocks and turned right again. When he parked in the middle of the block he saw the three men walk across the intersection in front of him. None of them looked his way. They had something in mind: they were looking for something, scanning the houses as they walked. Paul locked the car and walked to the corner and watched from there, staying next to the building where he could curl back out of sight if one of them looked over his shoulder.

Crubb was talking and the performance involved a great deal of body expression: his shoulders and arms and hands moved in great balletic patterns; with his friends he was a different creature from the prisoner in the courtroom. From a block away it was impossible to tell what he was talking about but his gestures expressed petulant complaint. Possibly he was expounding on the injustice of his arrest.

They passed a small apartment building without a glance;

65

they were studying the detached houses across the road. One of the men passed something heavy from his coat pocket to Crubb—perhaps a tool, perhaps a weapon. Crubb pushed it under his tight leather coat and held it there, one hand inside the lapel.

Paul stayed where he was; it was as good a vantage point as any, at least until they went a block or two farther. There were no other pedestrians on the street; a plumber's van went by but when it was gone nothing else moved in the street except Crubb and his two friends.

They were looking at the garages, Paul discovered. Looking for an empty one?

Then as if on random impulse they turned the corner and went out of sight. Paul hurried down the street.

It began to snow: large slow flakes. Paul turned his collar up. When he reached the corner he walked straight across the intersection, merely glancing both ways as if to make sure there was no traffic. The three men were jive-walking down the sidewalk peering at garages; one of them glanced back and Paul quickly looked the other way and kept walking until he'd interposed the corner house between him and their line of sight. Then he doubled back and peered carefully around the edge of the house.

The two companions stopped and Crubb walked up a driveway and cupped both hands to look through a window into a closed two-car garage. He shook his head and rejoined the others and they moved on.

Paul was sure of it now. They were looking for an empty garage: a sign that no one was home.

They were walking away from him but he saw Crubb's head turn—an instinctive wariness toward the backtrail. Paul swiveled back out of sight before Crubb had a chance to see him. He gave it a few seconds and then reconnoitered cautiously.

They had nearly reached the end of the block. Crubb poked a finger toward a house on the near side of the street; it was set back and Paul couldn't see it. All three of them crossed the street.

There was only one thing to do. He went back across the intersection, retracing his own path. None of them looked his way; they were intent on the house. From the south corner he could see the edge of it and the garage into which Crubb was peering. Crubb made a quick hand motion and all three men disappeared into the passage between houses; the third man paused to look both ways and Paul faded back. When he looked out again they were gone from sight. They'd be checking out the house before breaking into it.

Paul crossed the intersection a third time and turned left and walked toward the house, looking for a place to post himself and ambush them when they emerged with their loot. On his palms the cold dampness of fear was an old familiar companion.

Ω

13

¶ CHICAGO, DEC. 24TH—Five men were shot to death yesterday in two separate incidents in Chicago, bringing to a boil the rapidly heating controversy over the disputed existence of a "vigilante" on the city's streets.

Early yesterday afternoon three separate residents of the Humboldt Park residential area telephoned police to report gunshots, bringing fast response by motorized patrolmen who discovered the bodies of three men in a passage beside the residence of Ernest Hamling, of 3046 West Hirsch Street. On and near the bodies were a cassette tape recorder, silverware, two cameras, a shotgun, a small battery-powered television set and other items identified as the personal property of Mr. and Mrs. Hamling, neither of whom was at home at the time of the shootings.

Announcement of the identities of the three dead men has been withheld by police pending further investigation and notification of relatives. It was revealed by a police spokesman, however, that one of the three men had been released on bail by the Cook County Criminal Court only that morning, pending trial on a charge of robbery and assault.

The three men were allegedly killed by bullets from a single .38 revolver which may have been the same weapon that has been credited with the deaths of five alleged criminals in recent days. Police ballistics laboratories have taken the bullets for analysis.

In a separate incident last night, two youths were shot to death on a South Side fire escape while allegedly escaping from an attempted burglary of the Lincoln-Washington Social Club. The youths, identified as Richard Hicks and John R. Davis, both 16, were found by the club manager, Sherman X, after several loud gunshots were heard; allegedly the youths had broken in through a rear window and had stolen the club's cashbox containing receipts from a benefit discotheque dance, and were shot while escaping down the outside fire stairs at the rear of the building. A police spokesman said, "We've analyzed the angle of entry of the bullets. They were fired up at the victims from the alley beneath."

The bullets have been identified tentatively as having been fired by a .45 caliber automatic pistol. Interviewed in his Headquarters office this morning, Police Captain Victor Mastro, in charge of the "vigilante" investigation in the Homicide Division, pointed out that the two South Side youths were not killed by the same weapon which reportedly killed the other eight "vigilante" victims. "But," Mastro said, "the modus operandi is very similar, you'd have to say. We can't rule out the possibility that the killer owns more than one gun."

Ω

14

HER EYES FLASHED angrily. She'd been waiting near the door; she stood up when Paul entered the courtroom. He was once again surprised by how diminutive she was: she hardly came up to his shoulder and he was not especially tall. She wore a light sweater with the sleeves pushed up casually above the elbows; a long plaid skirt that was mainly orange and yellow; she'd done something with her hair and it was softer and fuller around her face than it had been yesterday.

"I'm not late, am I?"

"Actually you're early. No—it's not on your account I'm breathing fire. Let's go, shall we? I need a drink."

He helped her into her coat and they went down the steps trying to avoid puddles and slushpiles left from last night's snowfall. She said, "I was supposed to try an aggravated assault and attempted murder case this morning. The bastard didn't show up."

"Jumped bail?"

"That's right. Eight hundred dollars bail. I fought it at the hearing—it was ridiculously low."

"Do they skip bail often?"

"Not so often that I'm used to it."

He held the car door for her and then went around to get in. "Where to?"

"Do you like German food?"

He didn't, especially, but he said he did and she gave him directions; they put the car in a multistory garage in the Loop and walked to the Berghoff.

They ordered highballs and Paul lit her cigarette from a restaurant matchbook. When the drinks came they touched glasses. "Merry Christmas," he said.

"Happy New Year." She drank and shuddered theatrically. "Hoo boy."

"A tough one?"

"Some of them bother you more than others," she said. "This one was a fairly vicious little bastard. I hate to imagine what he's up to now."

In the gentle restaurant light she had a softer prettiness than he'd remarked yesterday. Her cheeks were high and freckled; she had a short nose and wide grey eyes. Her bones were prominent and she was curiously rangy—that was what made her seem much taller than she was.

She blew smoke through her nostrils. "I feel awkward. It's not a habit of mine, making dates with strangers. I did it on impulse, you know."

He smiled to reassure her. "So did I."

"Have you ever been to a psychiatrist?"

He was taken aback. "No."

"Neither have I. I wonder what a shrink would say about my 'motivations.' I've never had a loved one mugged. I've never even been burgled. But when I passed the bar exams I went straight into the DA's office and I've been there ever since. I've never been able to picture myself as anything except a prosecuting attorney. I never had the slightest urge to defend the downtrodden and support the underprivileged. It's strange because I don't think of myself as a redneck. I'm not politically right-wing at all. I don't know. Right now I'm in one of those agonizing reappraisals about the people I have to deal with every day. I've started asking myself whether there's any possibility of a society surviving without the things we think of as the old traditional civilized values. Personal dignity, respect for the law."

She wanted a sympathetic ear; he didn't interrupt.

"I've never believed crime was an illness that could be cured by treatment. Maybe one day we'll be able to go into them surgically and program new personalities and send brand new good citizens out into the world. I'd rather not live to see that either. But in the meantime I keep hearing about rehabilitation and reform, and I don't believe a word of it. The law isn't *supposed* to rehabilitate people or reform them. You can't force people to behave themselves. You can only try to force them not to misbehave. That's what laws are for. The humanitarians have forced us into this illogic of reforms and rehabilitations, and all they've succeeded in doing is they've created an incredible increase in human suffering."

"Crime isn't a disease to be treated," Paul suggested. "It's an evil to be punished."

"It's more than that," she said. "It's not just an evil to be punished. It's an evil to be prevented."

"By deterrence?"

"By getting them off the streets and keeping them off the streets." She lit another cigarette, inhaled, coughed, recovered and said, "Protections keep expanding for the rights of the accused. What about the rights of society to be free from criminal molestations?"

73

She went on, "The 'we're all guilty' approach used to mean something to me. You know: 'As long as one man anywhere is not free, *I'm* not free.' It's a great argument for doing away with prisons. But it's no good. *I* haven't committed atrocities. I'm not guilty of the crimes I have to try in that courthouse. I've never mugged anyone. There's a difference between me and them—we're *not* all the same. And if we haven't got the confidence and courage to make these moral judgments and act on them, then we deserve every dismal thing that happens.

"These kids from the Legal Aid hang around our office talking high-minded idealism. They keep talking about the causes of crime. What causes? I've heard ten thousand. Families have broken down. Unemployment. The evaporation of religion. Violence on television. Welfare. Corruption in high places. Racism. Poverty. Abnormal genetic chromosomes. That marvelous word 'alienation.' Permissive parents. The laws are too lax, or the laws are too severe—take your choice. Rootlessness, the breakdown of a sense of community, overpopulation, underachievement, drugs, too much money, too little money. Moral decay and disrespect. Pornography. What's the cause of crime? Every crime has its own causes. Every defendant I try has a marvelous excuse of some kind. But when the Nazis mobilize and arm themselves and invade your country, you don't ask why—you defend yourself and leave the causes to the historians."

"Yes," he murmured. He didn't dare say more.

"That's what I've believed for years," she said. "It's what I still believe. But I've begun to wonder whether it matters a whole lot what I believe."

"Why? Because you can't do much about things?"

"No. I do as much as I can. I suppose you could say I do more than most people do."

"Then what's bothering you?"

"It's so accidental, isn't it. I could just as easily be one
of those Legal Aids in the outer office. My best friend in
law school took a job with the Civil Liberties Union."

"It's like that line in the Western movies," he said, echo-
ing the words he'd said to Spalter. "You play the cards
you've been dealt."

"It depresses me to think maybe that's all it is. A chance
turn of the cards. An accident, no more significant than a
bet on a horse." She put her glass down; she hadn't drunk
much of the second one. "I feel as if I've lost something
important. Should we get menus and order something?"

Later she said, "I'm sorry. I haven't been much help to
either of us, have I."

"I didn't know we were expected to give each other ther-
apy." He smiled. "You're good company, you know."

"Actually I'm horrid today. I hope you'll forgive me—I
don't usually behave so badly."

He shook his head, denying it. "Do you have children?"

"No. I'm not married any more. I was for a while, but
as they say it didn't work out. Maybe it was my fault. I'm
not the homemaker sort."

"I wasn't trying to pry."

She put her knife and fork on her plate. "Why do you
and I keep apologizing to each other?"

"Nerves." He tried to smile. "I don't know about you.
But I haven't done much—dating." Well there'd been one
woman in Arizona, very briefly.

He wanted to change the subject. "What are your plans
for the evening?"

Amusement narrowed her eyes. "It's Christmas Eve," she
said, "and I thought you'd never ask."

15

¶ CHICAGO, DEC. 26TH—In a bizarre Christmas Day tragedy, a man who tried to rob Santa Claus was shot to death yesterday outside a church on Lake Shore Drive.

Witnesses leaving the First Methodist Church described the events. Claude Tunick, 54, dressed in a Santa Claus costume, was collecting donations on the sidewalk for a Methodist crippled children's fund. At 12:45 p.m. the noon Christmas Service inside the church came to an end, and the first worshipers to leave the building were in time to see a youth with a knife in his hand accost Mr. Tunick and wrest the cylindrical donations box away from him. Several of the witnesses ran down the church steps, trying to catch the thief or frighten him off.

Suddenly a shot was fired. Witnesses have been uncertain where it was fired from; most of them believe it was fired from a passing automobile which then sped away. The bullet struck Mr. Tunick's assailant, William O. Newton, 17, in the chest. Newton died less than twenty minutes later in an ambulance en route to city hospital.

A police spokesman said the death bullet had been fired from a .45 caliber automatic pistol. Ballistics technicians are comparing it with bullets of the same caliber which yesterday were reported as having killed two alleged burglars on the South Side.

"If the bullets match up," the spokesman said, "we'll regard it as a strong indication that the vigilante is still in operation. He may have traded in his .38 revolver for a heavier .45."

The vigilante—whose existence is still disputed in some official circles—has been accused of at least eight killings in Chicago in the past week, all of them involving the deaths of convicted or suspected felons. If the three .45 caliber homicides can be linked to the eight committed with a .38 caliber revolver, it will raise the vigilante's death toll to eleven.

Captain Victor Mastro, in a telephone interview last night, said, "Eleven homicides in a week isn't unusual for Chicago, unfortunately. Sometimes we have eleven in a single day. But if all of these have indeed been committed by one man, then it's not too strong a statement to say we've got a one-man murder wave on our hands. We're doing everything in our power to locate and arrest whoever is responsible for these killings, whether it's one man or half a dozen."

Captain Mastro, of the Homicide Division, is in charge of the vigilante case. His closing remark may have been in reference to several heated statements made lately by members of civil rights organizations, religious leaders, spokesmen for community groups, and two members of the Chicago Crime Commission, one of whom, Vincent Rosselli, spoke up in a County Council meeting on Tuesday, demanding "an end to vigilante terrorism in the streets of Chicago."

16

HE MET HER for cocktails at the Blackstone; she was at a table reading a newspaper. She was in her working clothes —the orange tweed suit he'd seen before. "How'd your exploring go today?"

"I did a couple of museums," he said. "No point driving around in this blizzard."

"Have you seen the papers?"

"Yes."

She put a fingernail on the vigilante headline. "It's got the machine in a real uproar."

"I imagine it would." He contrived to make his voice casual. "Do you want another one of those?"

"Not just yet."

He ordered scotch and water. The waitress repeated the words in a heavy French accent and went away wiggling the tail of her bunny costume.

"I spent half the day in the Museum of Science and Industry. You could get lost in that place." He'd been looking for muggers in the dark corridors where they liked to prey on wandering teen-agers and old women.

"I keep wondering if it isn't one of our esteemed mayor's crazy stunts."

"What's that?"

"The vigilante," she said. "It could be a cop, you know."

"I suppose it could be."

"Or the whole thing might be a phony. Suppose it's something they've cooked up in the crime lab? The victims could have been shot by eleven different guns, for all we know— we've only got the crime lab's word for it that there are only two guns involved. Suppose every time they find a dead man with a criminal record, they pin it on the vigilante?"

"Why would they do that?"

"Mastro was in court today to testify in a case. He told me—"

"Who?"

"Vic Mastro. He's a police captain, they've put him in charge of the vigilante case."

"Oh that's right," he said vaguely. "I knew I'd seen the name somewhere."

"Mastro said something interesting. You know cops, they've got an interstate grapevine like everybody else. He's got a friend on the force in New York. They're still blaming murders on the vigilante there."

"Yes, I know. They haven't caught him yet."

"He's been blamed for three killings in the past two weeks in Manhattan. Mastro thinks they're phonies. All three were shot by different guns. But the police are keeping the vigilante alive."

"You mean he's dead?"

"Nobody knows. But as long as the vigilante gets publicity, the crime rate stays down."

"Is it really down? There was a lot of debate about that when I was still in New York. The police and the mayor's office denied there'd been much change."

"They had to. Otherwise they'd be admitting the vigilante was accomplishing what their own police department couldn't accomplish. The fact is, street crimes were off almost fifty per cent for a while. They've started to climb again, but it's still far below the record rate. Mastro insists they're keeping the vigilante myth going for that reason."

Paul reached for the scotch when the waitress took it off her tray. "What's happened to the crime rate here in Chicago?"

"Down about twenty per cent in the past few days."

"Well it might be a policeman," he said. "Or a small secret group of policemen." He lit her cigarette for her; he'd taken to carrying matches with him. "Let's talk about something a little less grim."

She smiled. "I'm sorry. I've gotten too used to taking my work home with me. What time is the party?"

"Seven. You sure you want to go?"

"It'll be a change from the faces I see around the courtroom."

"They're probably crashing bores."

"We can always leave early."

The car had been manufactured before the introduction of interlocks or seat-belt buzzers and she perched next to him on the middle of the seat. He was pleased and he was alarmed. There was too much conflict in his reactions to her. He had contrived to cement the acquaintance because he needed to know more than the newspapers could tell him about the official hunt for the vigilante: every item of knowledge would help him stay ahead of them. Now that he knew she was on good terms with Mastro he knew he had to go on cultivating her. At the same time he liked her and

81

that was dangerous because he could not afford ever to relax with her.

He waited in the living room of her apartment while she changed behind the bedroom's closed door; he sipped a drink and read about himself in the *Tribune*.

"That's lovely," he said when she appeared. Pleased, she pirouetted for him; Paul laughed at her. At the awning on the sidewalk he opened the umbrella and convoyed her to the car under it; then they were driving north in a crawling tangle of half-blind cars, wipers batting the snow.

"You're a very careful driver."

"I lived all my life in New York. This is the first car I've ever owned. I've had a license since I was eighteen but I've never particularly enjoyed driving."

"Maybe that's why you're still alive."

He had to counter the impulse to look sharply at her. She'd said it cheerfully enough; she meant nothing by it. But her eyes in repose had something near a mischievous expression and at times he had the odd feeling she was amused by him: the feeling that she could see his every thought. It was a fantasy but it unnerved him; she was a clever woman and that implied peril.

She fumbled a cigarette from her bag and dropped it and Paul nearly panicked when she began to feel around on the floor for it. Suppose her hand touched the .38 that was clipped to the springs under the seat?

She found the cigarette and punched the dashboard lighter.

"I'm not sure whether that thing works."

"We'll find out soon enough."

The lighter clicked and she put the red end to her cigarette. "For shame. You didn't test it before you bought the car?"

82

"I kicked the tires. Isn't that enough?" *Get a grip on your-self.*

Childress lived on Clark Square in Evanston. The square was a park that fronted on the lake; three sides were faced by stately old houses and big trees heavy with snow arched over the street. It had a kind of decaying dignity like parts of Riverdale he'd seen.

They picked their way under the umbrella, skirting drifts and puddles. In front of the house a small car was parked. "That's Childress's car. Spalter told me about it."

"He does have a sense of humor, doesn't he."

The bumper sticker was large and bright-hued: "Be American—Buy American." The car was a Datsun.

The lawns were the sort that in the spring would bloom with azaleas and rhododendrons. You'd probably see children riding their bikes along the shaded sidewalks. Northwestern University was close by; doubtless some of the deans lived here; it was an odd neighborhood for an executive like Childress who routinely was described by flacks as "towering" but Spalter had explained that Childress had been born and raised in the house and had never entertained thoughts of moving to a more expensive area. Paul wondered how it would feel to live with his roots as solidly implanted as that; he had spent his own life adrift from apartment to apartment, driven from neighborhood to neighborhood by the constant shifts in New York's ethnic and economic boundaries. He couldn't remember having had anything like a home in the apple-pie Hollywood sense. It wasn't a lack for which he'd ever pitied himself but at times he was curious about it and the old-glove comfort of Childress's Victorian house brought the feeling to the surface.

It was a center-hall house with matter-of-fact staircase and carpeting that had seen wear. A maid admitted them:

83

she wore an aproned uniform that put him in mind of old movies. Gusts of laughter and talk came along the hall. Paul noticed the windowpanes were striped with electronic alarm tape.

Childress and Spalter appeared behind a woman in the far doorway; the three of them advanced smiling and there was a round of introductions and handshakes. The woman proved to be Childress's wife. She was a middle-aged club-woman, inclined to fat, grimly corseted; Paul had a glimmer of the motivation behind Childress's disapproval of corporate wives.

Childress's red round face smelled of expensive aftershave. He was very happy to meet Miss Evans. "Come and meet the rest of my sycophants." Childress's humor had bite; it was his defense against whatever demons he had.

"You know Jim Spalter, of course. He lives around the corner, now, fourteen blocks from his house—community property, you know."

The drawing room was larger than the exterior of the house had suggested. Against its defiantly staid musty furnishings there were vaguely erotic paintings and gay Japanese-style lights suspended at random levels from the ceiling; Paul was sure Childress had done it all with a straight face. As they entered the room Childress was buttonholed by a compatriot and waved them toward the bar as he turned his back; Irene said to Spalter, "My God, is he always like this?"

"You should see him at convention luncheons. You've never seen such an earnestly broad-minded prude. Anxious as hell to have everybody know he's a regular fellow."

"And sneering at them all the time out of the side of his mouth."

"That's the cross a genius bears."

84

She said to Paul, "You're going to have fun, if you don't cave in." She was twinkling.

"It's a new and different experience," he agreed drily. "I've never worked for a madman before."

Spalter said, "What'll you have?"

"A hangover, I expect," Irene said, "but I'll risk a bourbon and soda."

"Paul?"

"Scotch and water, thanks."

Spalter turned his back and pried his way to the bar.

An old man whose neck bulged with loose folds of fat came through the crowd beaming. He wore a grey striped suit, the baggy pants of which were cinched high around his chest like a mail sack. "Irene for Christ's sake."

"Harry—dear Harry, it's been so long. Paul, this is Harry Chisum. He's responsible for the abysmal breed of lawyers Northwestern turns out every year."

"Not any longer, dear. Professor emeritus since September."

"Oh Harry, no! They can't put you out to pasture."

"But they have."

"Harry was my mentor," she explained to Paul. "Major professor, goad and confessor."

Paul said he was happy to meet Professor Chisum and the old man shook his hand warmly. "Imagine a pupil of mine descending to the primeval slime of a Childress orgy. My dear I'm dismayed."

"And what are *you* doing here then?"

"Ah, I'm a perverted old lecher, didn't you know? A closet degenerate." He leered toward an enormous oil canvas of sated nymphs. "They sold those under the counter during the Italian Renaissance. Actually John Childress was one of my first students, you know. And still one of the

85

best, although no one remembers he was a lawyer before he turned his talents to the machinations of commercial accounting. The best—which is to say the most evil—businessmen are lawyers."

"And the worst lawyers are businessmen."

"It's not fair to throw an old man's words back at him. You've altogether too good a memory."

Spalter arrived balancing the drinks, distributed them and hovered. Irene said, "I can't imagine you playing shuffleboard. What are you doing with yourself?"

"What do retired intellectuals do? They stay out of mischief by writing books."

"Is it a secret?"

"Not from you. In any case it's the same book everyone's writing nowadays. I hope to offer a thing or two the others can't match. It's on crime."

"I'm dying to read it, Harry."

"I'd be delighted to have you pick holes in the manuscript. When it's completed."

"You know I'd be honored."

Spalter said, "I hope you've got some solutions for us, Harry. We've had enough experts expounding on what the problem is."

"I'm hoping that's the little difference that will single out my modest tome. It's not a book of questions. It's a book of answers."

Irene smiled her slow smile. "Harry, you can't just let that one lie on the floor like a piece of raw meat."

The old man was delighted. "You'll just have to wait and read the book, won't you." He nudged Paul. "I've got a sure sale already, you see?"

"Harry," she said firmly.

Paul said, "If you've got real solutions to the—"

"Answers, I said. Not solutions. A solution is that which

provides actual resolve of a problem. An answer, on the other hand, may be mere theory or hypothesis."

"You're still wriggling, Harry."

"The distinction is valid, my dear. My book can do no more than offer recommendations. They are recommendations which I'm certain the politicians and the public will find unacceptable if not repellent. They won't solve the problem, because they'll never be put into practice."

"My goodness. You sound as if you're going to propound something Hitlerian."

"Perhaps it is—if only to the extent that anything smacking remotely of authoritarianism is equated these days with Hitler."

"You can't kid us," Spalter joked, "we all know you're the vigilante, Harry."

Paul tried not to stiffen.

"That's Harry's secret solution," Spalter confined to Paul. "The Final Solution."

"Vigilantism solves no problems," Chisum said.

"Well it seems to be doing a pretty snazzy job with our crime rate right now, you've got to admit that," Spalter said.

Irene laughed in her throat. "I'm sorry. I'm just visualizing Harry skulking in a slum alley with two guns in his holsters. 'Draw, you varmint.' "

Paul managed a weak smile.

Spalter said, "I'll tell you one thing. Real or phony, this vigilante has stirred up the public consciousness like nothing you'd believe. Nobody talks about anything else. He's got a lot of sympathy out there. You talk to people around town, you begin to realize their feelings about things. Right or wrong, this vigilante is making people feel there's some kind of justice in the streets for the first time in memory. God knows it's a sudden justice, but all the same it's—"

87

"It's not justice," the old law professor snapped. "Whoever these vigilantes are, they've gone far beyond justice. They don't want justice. They want blood."

"They?" Irene said.

Spalter said, "It can hardly be the work of one man. Not all of it. New York and Chicago at the same time?"

Paul spoke, because it would have been strange if he hadn't. "You're suggesting he's—they've—got a thirst for blood. A hunger for violence and killing. I don't think that answers it, not completely."

Irene said, "I think Paul has a point. Revenge is a very personal thing, while justice is a social thing. But the vigilante—he or they, whatever it is—the vigilante has made a public issue of it. Deliberately. These murders are a public-relations campaign, in a way, and whoever's doing it wants to make it far more than just a private vendetta. He's trying to arouse the entire citizenry. He's trying to focus public concern on a crisis, and if you ask me he's doing a bloody brilliant job of it. No, I can't agree at all that it's pure blood sport or private vengeance."

Chisum shook his head; the folds of wattled flesh shook beneath his chin. "These men, the vigilantes, they're trying to act out their own personal fantasies of an ancient myth. The vigilante sees himself as some kind of reincarnation of the traditional American hero. I'm sure of that. He's got an image of himself as a messianic reformer, trying to resurrect the kind of heroism that forged our national identity in the Wild West. The frontiersmen who killed and got killed until the wilderness was mastered. But it was a false image then and it's false now. It wasn't the gunslingers who tamed the country. It was the settlers. In the same way, it can't be the vigilantes who'll solve anything today. They only add fuel to the flames."

The old man was at home with an audience. Other conversations around them had dwindled; people were turning to listen to him; Chisum's enthusiasms waxed visibly. His gestures grew larger. "These vigilantes may think they're doing something for society, but they're only acting out their own pathetic fantasies. Look. If there's a heavy snowstorm and a big building collapses, it's no good blaming the blizzard. You've got to go after the architect who designed the building. You've got to try and persuade him to change his architectural system.

"That's our problem. The architects are immobilized by outdated archaic traditions—the millions of laws on the books. And too many architects have been corrupted, they cut corners with cheap bulding materials and substandard contruction standards. That's the plea-bargaining system, the cops and judges who sell themselves as casually as streetwalking whores.

"And the public? The public is the buyers and renters of the building. They don't want to see enough money spent to insure a sound structure. They'd rather cut corners and take a chance there won't be a blizzard."

Spalter said, "You can't really say the public doesn't give a damn. What about this hue and cry about crime?"

"People are concerned that the building might collapse. But they don't act on that concern. The most widespread disease in this country is the sense of personal powerlessness. Impotence. It breeds apathy, and apathy breeds the violence of crime and vigilantism. The more powerless people become, the more violent they become—revolutionaries are always the powerless people."

"These criminals and vigilantes," Paul said. "Are they revolutionaries?"

"I think their motives are the same, essentially. They're

89

disaffected by their powerlessness and they're seduced by violence because it's the only way they can express anger with their frustration and impotence."

Paul saw John Childress nearby. Childress was smiling. "Harry, take a bow. You're doing a spectacular job of belaboring the obvious."

Chisum regarded his host with arch good-humored contempt. "The obvious becomes less obvious, John, when you consider the fact that we're completely stymied by two opposing forces—and that both of them come from exactly the same political source. One: the obsession with bringing in the government to correct every last flaw in the human condition. Obviously that makes the government more and more powerful, and the citizens less and less powerful. Two: the pathological fear of a possible misuse of power. The checks and balances.

"You see?" he demanded. "First we create a government with ever increasing power. Then we spend every waking hour finding ways to prevent that power from being used against us. It's total stalemate."

"Nothing can happen from the top, you mean," Spalter said.

"Right now it's only happening from the bottom, isn't it. Crime—and vigilantism."

"Then what's the answer?"

Chisum waved his age-spotted hands as if parting waves in a bathtub: deprecating, dismissing, minimizing. "The answer is the old human answer which we're too sophisticated to believe. Common sense. The democratic simpleminded fundament: the greatest good for the greatest number."

"Harry," John Childress said, "kindly eschew obfuscation."

90

"The answer consists, my brilliant warped friend, of a complicated combination of simple obvious reforms."

"To wit?"

"My book will list them all. I'll give you a few examples."

The professor held up his hand and lifted one finger at a time in enumeration.

"One. Stop arresting drunks. They're hurting nobody but themselves.

"Two. Stop arresting gamblers, prostitutes and the perpetrators of all other so-called victimless crimes.

"Three. Stop arresting drug addicts. Make narcotics cheap and easy to buy—on a par with alcohol and tobacco. This one always causes outraged indignant screams, but it's only common sense. It won't eliminate addiction. Nothing will. But it will eliminate crimes that the addicts commit in order to get money to buy the drugs that feed their habits. If they can get drugs cheaply they won't need to mug us. I submit that's more important than the self-inflicted 'crime' of addiction itself. If your son becomes a drug addict, that's his problem. But if he robs me to get money to buy drugs, he makes it my problem. I seek to eliminate my problem by making his drugs available to him cheaply. It's that simple. I'm not solving *his* problem—his addiction is a medical problem and that's between him and his doctor—but I am solving *my* problem, and, by extension, society's.

"Four. Tax every American citizen the sum of twenty dollars. With the money obtained, build prisons and courtrooms and staff them. Eliminate the bargained plea, the money bail system, and all systems of probation, parole and suspended sentences, except in extraordinary cases where there are abundant mitigating circumstances. Segregate these new expanded prisons according to severity of offense, in order to prevent hardened criminals from influencing minor offenders. Reduce penalties for minor infractions, but in-

91

crease penalties for major offenses, and make them uniform. Take the power to set sentences out of the hands of judges and make the sentence for each offense depend on the crime, not the judge. In other words, five years—no flexibility— for *any* armed robbery first offense, and fifteen years for *every* second armed robbery and life imprisonment for *every* third offense. Why? Not to punish, not to rehabilitate, not to reform. But simply to keep the offenders isolated from society where they cannot victimize us again."

Spalter interrupted him: "What about the death penalty?"

"The only remote justification for the death penalty is the economic one. It is cheaper to execute a man than it is to sustain him in prison for life. But the value to society of life imprisonment only holds water when it really means life imprisonment—not seven years with time off for good behavior.

"Incidentally there's good reason to reduce the penalty for most murders. Most homicides are committed within families—husband against wife, that kind of thing. The likelihood of the murderer's ever repeating his crime is usually remote; the crimes are committed in unique moments of passion, and anyway a woman who knowingly marries a man who killed his previous wife has to know the risk she's running. I'd say five years in prison would be a sensible penalty for internecine homicide."

"Where do vigilantes fit into your scheme?" Irene asked.

"Premeditated murder outside the family group," he answered promptly. "If convicted, mandatory life imprisonment. Or the death penalty if society prefers."

"A lot of people would disagree with that," Spalter said. "A lot of people would rather have the vigilante run for mayor."

The room broke up in laughter.

Paul said to Irene, "I see where you got some of your ideas."

Childress had an arm around the professor's shoulders; he was walking Chisum toward the bar, talking with sarcastic emphasis. The crowd milled and reformed its earlier knots of conversation and Paul heard words like impractical, visionary, sensible, utopian, cops, muggers, judges, lawyers, crime, prison, safety, civil war. And, he heard, vigilante.

Ω

17

¶ CHICAGO, DEC. 28TH—Two 14-year-old boys were slashed to death late last night by a 64-year-old man whom they are accused of having tried to rob.

The boys, Richard White, of 6513½ S. Paulina, and Michael Hayes, of 7418 S. Hermitage, cut with a kitchen knife in an alley near Kostner and Van Buren, fled from the alley and ran nearly 200 feet on Van Buren before they collapsed. Both boys died of their wounds almost immediately thereafter.

Captain William Marlowe, Commander of the Shakespeare District, said the two boys were looking for a mugging victim when they encountered Jorge Carrasquillo, 64, on Van Buren Street shortly after midnight. Mr. Carrasquillo had been drinking in a bar on Cicero Avenue and was homebound, on foot. Captain Marlowe has asked that Mr. Carrasquillo's address be withheld to avoid harassment.

Allegedly the two boys forced Mr. Carrasquillo into the alley, where White acted as a lookout while Hayes tried to take Mr. Carrasquillo's watch and money at gunpoint.

Mr. Carrasquillo wrested the gun, which later proved to be a toy, away from his assailant, and according to the police he then drew a kitchen knife from his coat pocket, cut Hayes across the neck, and then whirled around and slashed White, first on the hand, then across the throat.

The two boys were pronounced dead upon arrival at Cicero Hospital after Mr. Carrasquillo summoned police and an ambulance from a nearby public telephone.

Mr. Carrasquillo was released on his own recognizance pending a hearing to determine the facts of the case. A spokesman for the Cook County Attorney's office said the prosecution would move to have the case ruled justifiable homicide.

According to Captain Marlowe, Mr. Carrasquillo started carrying the kitchen knife with him only three days ago. "He said he'd decided to do it after hearing about the vigilante," Captain Marlowe said.

18

A SPIRAL of potato skin hung from the paring knife. She sat on a straight chair and her feet barely touched the floor. "I warn you right now. I always have been, am, and probably will continue to be a lousy cook."

Paul manhandled the cork out of the bottle. "Glasses?"

"Up there." She stabbed the knife toward the cabinet. "No, the next one. I think that's why he divorced me. Too many burnt hamburgers while I was working on a brief instead of inventing five-course feasts. But I got my revenge. He's gained twenty pounds since the divorce. I, on the other hand, remain as you see—malnourished or svelte, it depends on your point of view."

"You look damn good to me."

"Well thank you kind sir. My goodness this is nice wine. At least two dollars a bottle, what?"

"At least," he said gravely. He held his glass up to the light. "My friend Sam Kreutzer used to go on for hours about the nose, the hue, the tongue, the palate. I never knew what the hell he was talking about."

"Neither did he. Blindfold those guys and they can't tell red wine from ketchup." She dropped the potatoes into the miniature cauldron. "You've got a surprising little sense of humor, Paul."

"Standard survival equipment for CPA's."

She opened the oven and looked at the meat thermometer and picked up her glass. "Let us retire to the drawing room, sir."

The apartment was tidy and small: it was three paces from the kitchenette to the couch. Bookcases hung cantilever from the walls; evidently she was a voracious and catholic reader—only one section contained law books.

She waved him away when he fumbled for matches; lit her cigarette with a table lighter and sat back peering at him through a smoke-induced squint.

He said, "Do you ever play poker?"

"No. Why?"

"You'd be a killer at it."

"Am I so inscrutable? I don't mean to be."

"I keep wondering what you're seeing when you look at me like that."

"A rather sweet guy who's still trying to get himself sorted out after the world fell down around his ankles. And, I might add, probably a pretty good poker player himself. Are you?"

"I haven't played in months."

"But you used to."

"Every Thursday. I held my own but I'm no Cincinnati Kid. It was just a social game—the same friends every week."

"Do you miss them? Your New York friends."

"Some of them. Sam Kreutzer. The office wit—sort of a

fledgling Childress. But I've never been much of a social animal, I guess."

The cat leaped to a bookshelf and began to clean a paw. It was a grey and white tiger—inobtrusive, vigilant. Paul said, "I like people, in small doses, but I don't need to have them around me night and day. I don't really know what it means to have the kind of close binding friendship people talk about. Well, Sam was damned kind to me when my wife died—he stayed close by, helped me keep things together. But that's courtesy, isn't it. I mean it didn't bother me that I'd be leaving those people behind by moving to Chicago."

"What about your daughter?"

"We were fairly close. At least I think we were. But we weren't friends, really. Parent and child—I was very protective, maybe too much so. Maybe possessive. It's hard to know."

"I'm the same way," she said. "I was an only child. Actually I feel privileged. Liking people, but not needing them desperately. It makes you much freer, don't you think?" She left the burning cigarette on the rim of the ash tray and picked up her wine; she said in a different voice, "But still it seems worth a lot more if you have a little love along the way."

Ω

19

THE WIND had blown the snow off the trees but it lay deep in Washington Park coated with a frozen crust. The roadways and sidewalks had been cleared after a fashion but the night's hard cold had left glazings of ice and two black women walked with slow care balancing their supermarket bags in their arms. On the bench Paul watched them from the edge of his vision, propping the newspaper against the wooden rail. Wind fluttered the corners of the newspaper and he could see the black women's breath. Beyond them, beyond the trees and the end of the park he could see the slum houses: porches rotting off, cardboard in the windows. Two young men near the edge of the park were throwing snowballs at passing cars.

The two women approached the sidewalk and prepared to cross the road but one of them slipped on the ice. Paul saw the parcels fall. Groceries from the split bags sprayed across the snow, sliding on the glaze. The woman got to her feet with her friend's help.

The two youths went toward them, tossing snowballs aside.

Paul folded his newspaper and slipped the glove off his right hand and gripped the gun in his pocket. He got to his feet and moved toward them.

The youths reached the women, who watched without expression—expecting anything. Paul moved from tree to tree, unnoticed, fifty feet away from them.

He saw one of the young men speak; the wind was wrong, Paul couldn't hear the words. The woman who had fallen nodded bleakly.

But her friend smiled a little and then the two youths began gathering the scattered groceries.

A taxi went by, tire chains jingling. The paper bags were beyond use, broken in shreds; the woman stuffed things in the pockets of her threadbare coat and the two youths gathered armloads: a box of soap powder, a chicken wrapped in transparent plastic. The four of them waited for a truck to pass and then went slowly across the road.

Paul watched, moving forward without hurry. They might be Good Samaritans. Then again they might be going along until they had the women in a more private place. The woman who still had her packages had a handbag slung from her shoulder and women who did that much shopping at one time probably had cash in their purses.

Cut-Rate Liquors. First Baptist Church. The four pedestrians turned off into a dismal street of attached tenements.

From the corner Paul watched them climb the porch. But then the two youths emptied tins and jars from their pockets, stacked everything neatly on the porch and went back down to the street. He heard one of the women call her thanks across the snow.

He turned away and walked back toward the park.

20

THE HOUSING on Cottage Grove Avenue was urban rede-velopment, squat three-story boxes, shabby and hideous. He walked slowly, crunching snow—a lone white man in a good middle-class overcoat: an invitation to thievery. He kept looking up at house numbers—a bill collector looking for an address?

In his hand the pocketed revolver sweated cold against his skin.

Kids were building a snowman. They watched him walk by.

A snowball hurtled from behind, went over his shoulder and crashed beyond. He wheeled. His fist tensed on the gun.

He said aloud, "For Christ's sake." He got down on one knee and scraped a snowball together and threw it at the kids, not hard. It fell short and the kids laughed. He managed a smile, turned away and walked on. *For Christ's sake take it easy.* But it was an unnerving place. The cheap modern boxes were so inhuman: there was less dignity in them than in any tenement; no possibility of any sense of belonging, community, home. An awesome architectural confirmation of human rootlessness. No one could have identity in a place like this.

He left the area, hurrying.

21

THE GIRL was nearly grown; she must have been at least thirteen but her father had her tightly by the hand. He was a big man, black-skinned, overcoat flapping in the wind. With her free hand the young girl held her hat, though it was battened to her head by a scarf tied round her chin. Together they executed careful negotiations of the ice slicks and plow-piled snow at the curb, stepping over it and crossing the street into the grey dusk.

The man in the beret followed them, and Paul followed the man in the beret: a pilgrimage from the pawn shop into the darkness.

Paul had been in his car watching the pawnshop. It had happened quickly; he'd hardly parked the car. The father and daughter had been in the shop when he'd arrived and he hadn't seen them enter but it was likely they'd carried something in with them—something they weren't carrying now—and that was what had attracted the man in the beret.

Paul hadn't seen that one either until the man had emerged from his post in the doorway beyond the pawnshop. There was no mistaking the fact he was following them; he put his own feet in the prints the father had left in the snow at the curb.

By the time the man in the beret stepped off the curb to cross the intersection the father and daughter had disappeared into the cross street beyond the movie house; the man in the beret was giving them a lead, possibly to avoid alarming them.

Paul crossed the street directly from his car, cutting across the man's path; he gained distance that way and at the same time made it look as if he was heading toward the movie house on the corner.

A man was up on a ladder changing the movable letters on the marquee: one X-rated double bill died, another was born. Paul walked under the marquee and pretended to examine the posters advertising the lewdness within. The man in the beret went past the foot of the ladder and turned into the cross street. Paul kept his back turned until the predator was gone; then he went straight across to the far side of the cross street before he looked left.

Father and daughter were picking their slow careful way home hand in hand. The man in the beret wore soft black shoes—possibly sneakers: they made no sound. His stride had lengthened; he would overtake them in the next block.

Paul stayed close to the buildings; he moved in spurts from shadow to shadow. He'd thought days ago of tennis shoes but he'd had to abandon the idea; they'd have been out of place with his clothing. He could afford to do nothing that might attract notice.

The man in the beret was not tall but he had long legs and Paul had gained no ground on him by the end of the first block. Father and daughter were two-thirds the way to the second intersection and the man in the beret was only a half dozen paces behind; all three walked on the opposite side of the street from Paul.

He had to cross under the street light but the man in the beret didn't look back.

Paul reached the curb and a car went across the intersection behind him, tires slithering a little: the temperature was a good many degrees below freezing and everything had hardened.

He took the right glove off and slid the naked hand into his pocket and formed it around the revolver's grip.

Before he entered the darkness he looked to his right along the cross street—a random glance—and it made him stiffen: the car that had crossed behind him was a police car, quietly cruising. But it kept moving away steadily and he thought, *All they saw was my back,* and then he turned to search for the father and daughter and the man in the beret.

They had disappeared: the street was empty.

He moved swiftly, almost running, precarious on the ice; after half a dozen strides he angled toward the long ridge of snow the plows had piled up along the curb; he ran awkwardly, overshoes plunging ankle-deep into the snow, but it was better than falling.

He was scanning the doorways across the street. The lights were all gone: stone-throwing and sling-shooting kids routinely used them for target practice in streets like this. Here and there a dim glow splashed from a window imperfectly curtained; but the dusk had given way to night and visibility was very bad.

He was making a racket but scaring the predator off was better than nothing. He plunged his foot deeper than it should have gone—a chuckhole in the street; he fell into the hard snow and his cheek banged against the crusted ice.

He had to take his hand out of his pocket to push himself to his feet and then he took the first step gingerly, not sure whether he might have hurt his ankle. It was all right and he moved on, fumbling for the revolver.

A scream: it had to be the little girl's voice. He searched the shadows. There was a strange whacking noise: loud, sudden; he couldn't make it out. He ran along the edge of the street. The girl began to scream again and he heard the hard slap of flesh against flesh; the scream was cut off abruptly in its middle.

It was close by him. Somewhere almost directly across the street. He left the snowbank and slithered across the iced asphalt, lifting the Centennial from his pocket. His face stung where he'd fallen on it.

The man in the beret leaped at him.

He came from a well beyond the stone railing of the front stairs: a single bound onto the curb, an immense weapon raised high overhead—huge, a great enormous blade.

Machete.

The man's eyes gleamed in the night. Paul lost his footing, went down, broke his fall with the heel of his left hand. The two-foot machete loomed above him, lofted in both hands: a wallet fell on Paul's leg. The man's bewildering cry thundered: *"Get that mother!"*

Paul fell back flat in the street: he fired.

The bullet caromed off something. It slid away with a sobbing sound.

Trigger and then trigger again. . . .

He was still shooting when the revolver was empty and the machete clattered on the ice and the man was falling across Paul's overshoes.

He dragged himself out from under, trembling uncontrollably. He got to his knees.

The man died with a blast of breath and a single twitch, and a stench that immediately expanded around him.

Paul crouched, staring at the dead man as if to prove to himself that he could take it.

Finally he stood, trying to breathe through the nausea. Around the body it was spreading, a great bloodstain like a psychiatrist's inkblot.

He stumbled toward the stone steps and peered into the darkness there. At the foot of the service stair, half a floor below ground level, the young girl stood huddled in the corner. Her face was slack with shock.

Her father sagged beside her, sitting down, his back to the stones, clutching an arm from which blood poured sickeningly. His chin was down on his chest; he was rocking himself in pain. He never looked up.

But the young girl stared upward and Paul thought, *She's seen me.*

Then when he moved her eyes didn't stir. He saw the glaze then, the unfocus.

She was blind.

That was why her father had held her so closely by the hand.

He heard a siren. He couldn't tell where it was or which direction it was going.

He reached up. The empty gun was still in his hand. He dragged the back of his hand across his cheek. Blood still dripped from the scraped side of his jaw where he'd fallen.

The girl was trying to speak to him but the siren grew louder.

Paul lurched away.

Ω

22

"AM I FORGIVEN?" He held the phone against the left side of his face and tentatively prodded the scab on his right cheek with a finger.

"Take a lot of Vitamin C," she said.

"Sam Kreutzer would have prescribed chicken soup."

"It couldn't hurt." Her voice was thin; it was a poor connection. "Are you sure I can't bring dinner over?"

"No, really, I'd just as soon not spread this cold around—especially to you. I'll call you tomorrow."

"Take care." She said it tenderly; then the line was dead. For a moment he continued to hold the receiver against his ear, as if to maintain the thread of contact with her.

He had a bit of a head cold but that was only the excuse. He'd broken the date because he didn't want her to see the scraped streaks on his face. Another day or two and he could pass them off as shaving cuts; until then he didn't want to be seen by anyone—especially by Irene. She was too close to the inside: she'd know just about anything the police knew, and she was quick enough to put things together if given the evidence.

Even the newspapers were speculating on the bloodstains found in the snow. The police were analyzing them.

If the blood found on the snow fails to match the blood types of the dead assailant and the injured mugging victim, Captain Mastro said, police believe they may be a step closer to identifying the vigilante.

They were jumping to the wrong conclusion, evidently. They thought the vigilante had been cut by the machete. But in any case they were assuming the vigilante was wounded and Paul intended to stay in the apartment until he looked presentable.

Analysis of powder stains on the dead man's clothing indicates he was shot at pointblank range. Angle of entry of the lethal bullets indicates the shooter was prone at the time of the killing. Had he been knocked down by a blow from the machete? Chicago police aren't saying. But Lloyd Marks and his blind daughter Joanne had something to say this morning when reporters were granted interviews in Marks' hospital room. "I hope he wasn't cut too bad," Marks told reporters. "Because all I can say is, thank God that man showed up when he did."

It was a break for him that the New York police had kept the "vigilante" alive there: five killings, attributed to him in the newspapers, had been committed in Manhattan and Brooklyn while Paul was in Chicago. But at some level of authority there were men who knew the truth. If those men in New York decided to be candid with their colleagues in Chicago it was possible that the Chicago police might begin to sift information about any New Yorkers who had moved to Chicago in the past few weeks. If that happened they could hardly fail to scrutinize him closely. They'd interview Spalter and Childress, they'd question the employees of his apartment building, and he had no doubt they'd get around to Irene. There was no way to allay suspicion entirely but he had to be careful far beyond mere circumspection; he had to be absolutely certain he'd left no clues at all. Suspicion was one thing; evidence another. All they'd need would be one scrap.

He had to be as expert as a consummate professional. Everything had to be thought out: every ramification had to be considered. It was like a chess game.

Amateur status had protected him. He was unknown to the professionals—both the detectives and the underworld. He had no criminal contacts; therefore no informer could betray him. He had no criminal record; therefore no dossier could pinpoint him. He had the tacit approval of an unknown number of police officers and the investigation was being pursued less enthusiastically than it would have been if he were a mad killer of random innocents. The vigilante terrorized no one except those who deserved it, in the eyes of the police and a good part of the public.

It wasn't hard to size up these factors dispassionately.

But there was another factor that was harder to deal with

Just twelve hours prior to the machete tragedy on the South Side, two Oak Park youths had been slain by bullets from a .45 automatic pistol while apparently in the act of stripping a parked car. (See story on page 11.) Yesterday's incidents, therefore, bring to fourteen the total death toll attributed to Chicago's vigilante— or vigilantes; police have not yet determined whether more than one mysterious perpetrator is involved. The repeated use, at seemingly random intervals, of two separate murder weapons may suggest there are two separate vigilantes, Captain Mastro said, but "doesn't necessarily prove it."

23

IN HIS fantasies he had dialogues. At first with Esther after she died; then with Carol after she'd been institutionalized. Now occasionally in daydreams he articulated his reasoning to Irene.

"Yesterday I killed another one."

"Why?"

"He had a machete. He was attacking a man and a blind girl."

"How many does that make now?"

"In Chicago?"

"Since you started in New York."

"I don't know. Twenty-five maybe. I don't notch my guns."

"Are you afraid?"

"I'd be weird if I wasn't."

The imagined dialogues followed a pattern but some-

times the wording changed; his fantasies refined and rehearsed fitfully.

"What scares you, Paul? What are you afraid of?"

"Death. Pain. The police. I don't want them to find out
who I am."

"Is that all?"

"Them. The ones in the streets."

"You're afraid of them."

"That's why we've got to fight them."

"Is it? Is that why you hunt them?"

"It started in blind anger. I wanted revenge. Retribution
for what they'd done to my wife and my daughter."

"But it changed?"

"There are still such things as good and evil."

"You see it as a crusade?"

"I don't know. I heard them talking about messianic
delusions. It's not that. I'm not trying to save the world.
I'm only trying to show people that they can defend themselves. They shouldn't have to live in terror every time
they step out the door."

"No, they shouldn't. But why should you take it upon
yourself?"

"Somebody's got to do it."

"That's a cliché."

"So?"

"It's not an answer to the question."

"I don't know how to answer it. I just do it."

"Put it another way. Killing them—how do you justify
that, in terms of good and evil? How do you justify murder?"

"Is it murder? Self-defense, execution, protecting the
rights of innocent people, wiping out a disease—you can
call it a lot of things besides murder. Even war. It's a kind
of war."

"You've killed unarmed people. Kids."

"Once I shot a kid who was climbing out a window with a television set in his arms."

"And you passed a death sentence on him. Was it a capital crime?"

"You can smell it. If anybody'd got in his way he'd have killed them without a second thought."

"Is that your answer?"

"If my actions have prevented a single innocent person from being killed by these animals, then I'm justified. That's my answer."

"There's something else, though."

"What's that?"

"It's not just something you do out of a feeling of duty."

"No. I do it because they scare me. I'm afraid of them and that makes me hate them. Hate—it's an honest feeling."

It went around in circles and he never found its ending.

24

¶ CHICAGO, DEC. 30TH—A violent double-homicide late last night in the Ford City shopping center may have provided Chicago police with their first important clue to the identity of the vigilante.

The killings took place at 11:20 p.m. when two hold-up men entered the Pizza Heaven counter restaurant, held five people at gunpoint while they cleaned out the cash register, and left the restaurant only to be cut down in a hail of bullets by a man in a car, firing a pistol from his open car window.

The assailant then drove away, but not before the people in the restaurant had seen his face.

Both holdup men were pronounced dead by a police surgeon who arrived only minutes later with an ambulance summoned by two motorized patrol officers who reached the scene only moments after the pizza chef, Henry Fino, telephoned the police.

A stolen car found parked within thirty feet of the restaurant is assumed to be the holdup men's intended getaway car; its engine was still running when police arrived.

Several Chicago reporters reached the scene quickly, alerted by code calls on police-band radios; they were in time to see Captain Victor Mastro arrive. Captain Mastro, chief of the Homicide Division's detectives, has been placed in charge of the special detail designated to investigate the vigilante cases.

Reporters were not permitted to interview the four patrons who had been at the counter in the restaurant at the time of the killings. Their identities were withheld by police, and the four witnesses were secluded immediately. The pizza chef, Mr. Fino, talked with reporters but his position in the restaurant during the shootings had been near the cash register at the rear and he had not seen either the vigilante or the car.

Mr. Fino said, however, that at least two of the four people at the counter had "seen the whole thing."

Captain Mastro told reporters that according to his preliminary reconstruction of the events, "It looks likely the vigilante was following them, tailing their car."

Asked why he felt that was the case, Captain Mastro explained, "Because otherwise it's too coincidental, his showing up just at the time they were backing out of the restaurant with the loot. We assume he either knew who the two men were, or had some reason to suspect their intentions. He must have tailed them into the shopping center parking lot, and arrived in front of the restaurant just as they finished emptying the till. He switched off his headlights until the two men left the restaurant. Then he turned the lights on, pinning

117

the two men in the headlight beams, and fired four times before they had time to know what hit them."

The two deceased holdup men have not yet been identified. Their fingerprints have been forwarded to Washington in the hope that FBI files will assist in identifying them. "They weren't Chicagoans," Captain Mastro said. "Probably a couple of drifters, passing through."

The two holdup men were armed with cheap "Saturday night special" handguns, neither of which had been fired recently.

Captain Mastro said, "When the assailant backed his car out and turned it around to drive away from the restaurant, his face was seen by at least two of the people in the restaurant. We have a description of him from these witnesses, and we're pressing the investigation vigorously on that basis."

The captain declined to state any particulars about the description obtained from the witnesses. Mr. Fino, however, said that to the best of his knowledge, the customers at the counter had not gotten too good a look at the man in the car. He said one of the witnesses had told him, "It looked like a white man with light hair—grey or blond or white hair. But that was about all she could see." That judgment would seem to be borne out by a cursory survey of the arrangement of lights in the shopping center parking lot; the face of a man sitting inside a car thirty feet from the front of the restaurant would be vaguely identifiable at best, according to experiments performed by reporters on the scene; and visibility was hampered by steam and smoke stains on the plate-glass front windows of the pizza restaurant, through which the witnesses are said to have seen the vigilante.

Police admitted that none of the witnesses was able to provide either the license number or even a usable description of the vigilante's automobile.

Fragments of four bullets removed from the two deceased hold-up men appear to have been fired by the same .45 caliber automatic pistol used in several previous killings attributed to the vigilante, according to the police.

"The ammunition, both in the .38 cases and in the .45 cases, has been expanding hollow-point ammunition," Captain Mastro said. "These dum-dum bullets tend to explode on contact, shattering into little fragments like shrapnel. Naturally this process makes it considerably more difficult to recover significant bullet sections and to subject them to identification analysis in the laboratory. I'm not trying to say it can't be done. It can be done, and we are doing it, but it takes longer and the results sometimes are not as conclusive as we'd like them to be. For example, in two cases involving these .45 bullets, we can't absolutely prove they were fired by the same weapon that fired all the others, although the circumstantial evidence suggests they were. We simply didn't recover enough lead that hadn't been smashed beyond recognition."

Captain Mastro revealed, additionally, that none of the expired empty cartridge cases have been recovered by police at the scenes of any of the killings. "In the case of the revolver that's not surprising, of course, since revolvers don't automatically eject their empty cartridge cases," Captain Mastro said. "But the .45 automatic ejects its brass each time it fires, and this means our man has been careful to stop and pick up his empties before leaving the scenes of his killings. Either that or he's done his shooting from inside his car, so that the empties are ejected into the car where he can collect them at his leisure."

Progress has been made in identifying the type and manufacture of the vigilante weapons, according to Captain Mastro. "We've found out in the laboratory what the make and model of the two handguns are. We're withholding that information for the moment, but we do have it."

Ω

25

"You're in a good mood, Paul."

"It's New Year's Eve. It comes with the territory." He gave her a friendly swat on a firm bouncy buttock.

Irene carried her drink to the window. The blinds were open; frost rimmed the edges of the plate glass. "It's a marvelous view from here. You're very lucky."

He moved to her; he felt her spine beneath his fingers. "Think of all the frantic parties tonight."

"I never go to those. A quiet evening for me. My God, kazoos and noisemakers and funny hats."

"And Auld Lang Syne and kissing everybody in the room."

"I'll go for that part," she said; she gave him a sideways look, up from under; she was laughing and he pulled her forward and kissed her, felt her mouth push out, relax and open.

Then she stood in the circle of his arms; she tipped her cheek against his shoulder. She was still looking through the glass. Her voice came up to him very soft, muffled by his shirt: "Count the millions of lights out there, and realize only one of them is yours. Does that bother you?"

"No. Should it?" Anonymity was his protection.

"You've got your ego well under control. That's one of the things I like about you."

He leered. "What are the others?"

"Oh no. I'm not going to enumerate all your excellences, Paul—why should I give you ammunition?" She escaped with an impish pirouette and went inquisitively around the room pausing here and there to hover near a photograph of Paul and Sam Kreutzer on shipboard, a hard-cover copy of *Plain Speaking*, a silk-screen copy of a Picasso etching no bigger than an index file card, the small collection between bookends of Paul's LP record albums: Karajan's Beethoven, the Swingle Singers, P.D.Q. Bach, Lizst, Goldmark, Peter Nero, Al Hirt.

"You look gorgeous and girlish in that little skirt."

"Well it's not exactly the right season for it but I thought a little frivolity was called for." But she was pleased by the compliment, clumsy as it may have been.

In his vague fantasies it was much too easy to see her making a warm serene home. He took her glass from her and went to refill them both; he felt unnerved.

She trailed him into the kitchen. "You really did a job on your face."

"I hadn't tightened the blade in the razor. Incredibly stupid. I did all this with one swipe before I realized the blade was loose."

"I'd better get you a cartridge razor."

"I bought one this morning." Actually he'd always used a cartridge razor but he'd bought a brand new one today and thrown the old one out. The first time she went in the bathroom she'd see the cardboard-and-plastic package on the rim of the wastebasket. It was the details, he thought; concentrate on every detail, get it right, forget nothing.

"What's this gizmo?"

"Trash compactor."

"My goodness. You've really got all the mod cons in this building. Dishwasher, compactor—is that a self-cleaning oven?"

"I'm waiting for the self-making bed."

"And the self-vacuuming rug. Wasn't there a Ray Bradbury story . . . ?" She accepted the highball and moved back into the living room. "What's your resolution for the new year?"

"I don't know. What's yours?"

"Haven't you noticed—I haven't had a cigarette all evening." She attacked her drink like an addict snatching an overdue fix: she made a comic act of it. "I'm going out of my mind with nicotine withdrawal."

"It'll get worse before it gets better."

"Were you a smoker?"

"Long time ago. I gave it up when the surgeon general started issuing threats."

"My God you're disgustingly virtuous. You don't smoke, you eat and drink in moderation. You haven't got anything to give up."

"I was thinking of giving up sex."

"Good Lord. Whatever for?"

"So that you could talk me out of it."

"How strong a case would I have to present?"

"Not very."

"That's what I thought."

"Turnips," he said triumphantly.

"What?"

"I'll give up turnips."

"You hate turnips."

"Exactly."

"Bastard. I'm getting no sympathy at all. Look at me. I've got the shakes, my eyes are watering, I'm knotted up with indescribable pain, I'm a complete and utter wreck with a ten-ton monkey on my back. And you're offering to give up turnips."

"How about Brussels sprouts?"

"I could kill you."

"No you couldn't," he said.

Ω

26

SHE LAY on her right side, hands under her cheek. He left the bed slowly because he didn't want to wake her; he went into the kitchen, slippers flapping along the floor, and went through the ritual of assembling utensils and ingredients to make the English coffee she liked—a mixture with warm milk.

Beyond the window the city was crystalline: the sky unusually deep, the buildings of the Loop colored crisply by the morning sun. It looked like a giant Kodachrome projection in very sharp focus.

He wondered how many revelers had died from knife or bullet.

He crossed to the front door and opened it and found the morning paper on the mat; he brought it in and shot both locks. The coffee was beginning to bubble. He unfolded the newspaper on the table.

He heard the shower begin to spray against its frosted glass door. He smiled a little and turned down the flame under the saucepan of milk.

The headline caught his eye.

DOES VIGILANTE INSPIRE VIOLENCE?

Two New Year's Eve incidents led Captain Victor Mastro of the Chicago police to comment last night that defensive violence in Chicago may be on the increase because of widespread publicity over the killings of the mysterious vigilante.

Talking off-the-cuff to reporters at the Police Commissioner's annual Open House for the Press, Captain Mastro referred to two incidents reported earlier in the day.

In one case, a South Side woman repelled a mugging attempt by two unidentified youths on populous Martin Luther King Boulevard. The woman sent the youths running after she fought them off with a heavy length of iron pipe which she had been carrying in her handbag.

In the other case, an attempted holdup of a filling station on Canfield Road in Norridge was thwarted by an attendant who took a loaded shotgun from its hiding place beneath the cash register and fired both barrels, apparently injuring both would-be robbers, although the two men got away in their car and are still at large. The gas station attendant was quoted as saying, "The vigilante's got it right, man, there's only one language these guys understand."

Captain Mastro said, "There's a danger in this kind of thinking. When an armed robber comes into your place of business, you run a tremendous risk if you resist him. A lot of these men are hardened criminals. Unless you're as tough and as expert with guns as they are, the chances are pretty good that you'll end up the loser if you get into a gun battle with them. It's our official policy to recommend against the possession of any deadly weapon, even if it's purchased purely for reasons of self-defense. It's too easy for people to get hurt or killed. A few dollars out of a cash register isn't worth a shopkeeper's life."

But when asked whether Chicago's street-crime rate had been reduced since the vigilante case began, Captain Mastro refused to comment. "Any answer to that question would be misleading right now," he said. "There are too many factors involved."

He carried the two cups of coffee into the bedroom. She came out of the bathroom naked, toweling beaded water off her shoulders. The ends of her hair were matted damp. She smiled—very warm and still a little sleepy.

"Happy New Year."

"It is." She dropped the towel and embraced him. Her skin was tight from the shower. He had a saucer and cup in each hand; he put them down carefully and closed his arms around her. Her kiss was soft and slow. "Thanks for making it the happiest one in a long time, darling."

She disengaged herself and went to her clothes; he watched the sway of her small round hips. He said, "There's coffee here."

"I think I'll wait. If I drink it steaming hot I'll only want a cigarette."

When he had showered and dressed they sat in the kitchen spooning segments of grapefruit and Paul said, "I don't have to report for work until Monday. That gives us five days.

Why don't we go away somewhere? How about New Orleans?"

"Oh I'd love that. I've never been to New Orleans. But I've got to be in court tomorrow and Friday."

"We'll do it another time, then."

"I'll hold you to it." She pulled the morning paper around. "Mastro again. My God, if this vigilante business goes on much longer he'll be the most famous cop in the country. Next thing he'll be running for President."

"What sort of guy is he?"

"He's all right. A good cop, really. He's got a brain and he still knows how to use it—he hasn't been anaesthetized by the bureaucracy. But nobody ever heard of him, outside of the professionals, until the vigilante case started. Now he's had a taste of what it means to be a celebrity, and I think he's learning fast how to make the most of it. Christ I'd like a cigarette. How can you read the morning paper without a cigarette?"

"You get used to it after the first ten or fifteen years."

"You're a fat help."

He had to tread gingerly. "The paper yesterday said he'd identified the vigilante's guns. I got the impression between the lines that he knows more than he's telling the public."

"That's the impression they want to give. They want the vigilante to think they're closing in on him. Actually they're no closer than they were the day it all started. They haven't got any leads at all."

"But what about those witnesses in the pizza place?"

"They saw somebody in a car at night. He had a gun in his hand and bullets were flying around. They saw it through a filthy window, from a brightly lit room, looking out into a dim parking lot thirty or forty feet away. What do *you* think?"

"Do they think it's just one vigilante or a bunch of them?"

"They haven't got any idea."

"Personally I'd guess it was just one guy," Paul said. "He's pretty clever, obviously. He must be clever enough to use two or three different guns just to confuse the police."

"Beats me," she said. "And it beats Vic Mastro too, I'm afraid. He wants to nail the vigilante—he knows how much it would do for his career. But he doesn't want it to happen too quickly. Vic wants to milk it for every ounce of publicity he can get before he finally marches up the City Hall steps with the vigilante in handcuffs."

"Do you think that will happen?"

"Eventually it's bound to. Sooner or later the vigilante will make a mistake. He may have made one already—the night he tangled with that nut with the machete. He may have been cut pretty badly. They're canvassing all the hospitals and private doctors within a hundred-mile radius. They may find him. If this one doesn't turn up any leads, the next one will. The vigilante has one fatal disadvantage. He only needs to make one mistake. That's all, just one, and he's finished. The police can make all the mistakes in the world. They only need to be right once."

"You make it sound cut and dried. Inevitable."

"It is, really. It's only a question of time."

"What if the vigilante just decided to retire or move on to some other town?"

"Who knows," she said. "The interesting question to me is, what happens if they do catch him?"

"What do you mean?"

"He's quite a hero to a lot of people out there. What happens if we have to put him on trial?"

"I see what you mean."

"We could have demonstrations—even riots. Nothing's

unheard of in this town. A vigilante trial in Chicago could turn into an incredible political football."

"I wonder how it would turn out," Paul said. "More coffee?"

Ω

27

THURSDAY MORNING he dropped Irene at her office and drove south into the slums. He spent the day prowling the inferior regions of the city but the extreme clear cold was keeping people off the streets and at half past two he went back toward the center of the city to carry out the next step in his plan.

He'd singled out half a dozen ads from the classified real-estate page and he looked at four of the offices until he found one that suited his purpose. It was on a backwater fringe of the Loop near the intersection of Rush and Grand Avenue. There were a parking garage, several woebegone shops, a bar, a porno-poster shop, and on one corner a vacant lot and beyond it a building undergoing demolition.

The ad led him to a three-story brick building old enough to be grimed with soot. A narrow passage between two store-fronts led him up a flight of steps. The superintendent had a cubbyhole on the landing; he was a bald man with a black monk's fringe above his ears, in need of a shave and a beer-free diet; he led Paul up another flight to the top floor.

The office was a single room. Its two filthy windows looked out upon Grand Avenue. It was offered as a furnished office: that meant it had a desk that looked as if it had been bought surplus from the army, a flimsy swivel-chair on casters with frayed upholstery, a dented filing cabinet, a gooseneck lamp on the desk, the threadbare remnants of a rug; the lamp and the ceiling fixture had no bulbs in them but someone had left half a roll of toilet paper on top of the filing cabinet. There was a coat closet—two bent wire hangers—and a legend on the frosted glass pane in the door had been badly scraped off, leaving enough paint behind to see that a previous occupant had been a novelty company. There was a black phone on the desk but the superintendent told Paul it would need connecting. The rent was eighty dollars.

Paul signed a six-month lease in the name of his deceased brother-in-law. He gave the superintendent one hundred and sixty dollars in cash for security and the first month's rent. At no time did Paul remove his gloves. He told the superintendent he ran a small mail-order business in personalized greeting cards; the superintendent showed no curiosity. He gave Paul keys to the outside door, the office door and the bathroom down the hall.

Paul said he'd had a fire in his previous building. He inquired about fire exits. The superintendent showed him the back stairs: fire stairs that went down to a steel door on the ground floor at the rear of the building. It gave out onto an alley cluttered with trash cans. You could open the door from inside without a key but you couldn't enter from outside without one; the outside had no handle and there were steel buffer plates grooved into the doorframe to prevent a burglar from slipping the lock with plastic or wire.

He spent the rest of the afternoon preparing the remainder

of his cover. He ordered cheap printed stationery and a few rubber stamps, mailing envelopes, a postage meter, a second-hand typewriter, a packet of stick-on address labels, a small bag filled with office miscellany: paper clips and ballpoint pens, cellotape, manila file folders. Then he went up State Street to a cord shop and bought twenty dollars' worth of assorted greeting cards.

He stopped at a public booth and called the telephone company; gave the name and previous address and phone number of his brother-in-law in New Jersey and asked the company to connect the telephone in his new office. The appointment was made for Monday morning.

Neuser Studios was born. At half past four he returned to the flyspecked office and distributed his office supplies, wearing rubber kitchen gloves he'd bought in a variety store on his way back from State Street. He slipped one greeting card into each manila folder and stacked them all in the filing cabinet. He set up the old typewriter on the desk and screwed light bulbs into the fixtures.

He'd spent nearly three hundred dollars including the rent and security. It was for the single purpose of establishing a hiding place for the guns.

He could no longer afford to have the guns in his apartment, nor even in his car when he left it unattended. When he began work at Childress his apartment and car would be empty all day long: suspicion might lead Mastro's troops in his direction and he could afford to take no chances; his apartment and car might be searched.

At the other end of the investigation it was possible they'd canvass arms dealers; there might be ten thousand .38 Centennials in the Chicago area but there was the remote possibility they'd question Truett in the Wisconsin gun shop and find out that Robert Neuser had bought the two pistols there. They'd start hunting for Neuser then. They'd find him listed in an office on Grand Avenue and they'd search the office, and they'd find the guns.

But they wouldn't connect Neuser with Paul. He must never leave a single fingerprint in the office or indeed anywhere in the building.

Or on the guns.

He cleaned both of them, oiled them and wiped them down. He wiped the cleaning kit as well; then put kit and both guns in the bottom drawer of the filing cabinet. It had no lock and there was always the chance a burglar would break into the place and steal the guns but if that happened it would do Paul no real harm; it might even provide a red herring for the police to chase, if the burglar used the stolen guns.

In any case he could always buy another gun.

When he returned to the street it was dark and the rush-hour traffic was diminishing. He got his car out of the parking garage and turned north toward Irene's apartment.

Ω

28

¶ CHICAGO, JAN. 3RD—A twelve-year-old boy shot and wounded his sixth-grade teacher yesterday when she scolded him for classroom misbehavior, Chicago police reported.

¶ CHICAGO, JAN. 3RD—When a robber with his hand in his coat pocket threatened to shoot a CTA bus driver if the farebox wasn't handed over, the bus driver shot him.

The robber proved to be unarmed.

The robber carried no identification. He died at County Hospital without regaining consciousness after emergency surgery.

"He said he had a gun in his pocket," said the driver, James Sweet, 31, of 3108 W. Beach. "I didn't aim to be another dead robbery victim."

CTA regulations prohibit transit employees from carrying guns. "But I'd rather be fired and alive than employed and dead," Sweet said. "As far as I was concerned it was my life or my job."

Sweet said he had been carrying the gun since he first heard about the vigilante.

The robber boarded Sweet's Number 46 bus on Western Avenue near Addison and began to threaten Sweet as soon as the doors closed, Sweet said. There were no other passengers on the bus. Sweet immediately activated the secret distress signal which has been installed on all CTA buses, but no police responded immediately to the alarm.

"He gave me no choice," Sweet said. "I don't carry a key to the farebox. I couldn't hand it over. And even if I could, why should I?"

Sweet has been a bus driver for seven years. "It's been getting worse and worse," he said. "Drivers get knocked over nearly every day now."

The robber, described as being in his early twenties, is being investigated through fingerprint identification.

A CTA spokesman said Sweet would not be suspended or dismissed immediately; a decision is forthcoming, he said, pending departmental investigation.

No criminal charges have been brought.

Ω

29

COOK COUNTY Juvenile Court was housed in a long flat dark building, square and stylelessly modern; it was five stories high and might have been a factory or a company headquarters, or a leprosarium. It fronted on the point of an acutely triangular block, bias-cut by the diagonal slash of Ogden Avenue.

Ogden's Route 66 truck traffic rumbled past steadily. Paul turned out of the stream and parked on Hamilton Avenue opposite the side entrance of the Juvenile Court.

The sky had thickened and gone pewter. Snow that had fallen in December remained in the park and on the curbs; there had been no thaw. At intervals while he waited he started the engine and ran up the heater until the interior of the car grew uncomfortably hot; then he sat in stillness while the cold pried its way through the sealed windows.

He had the newspapers on the seat beside him; he went through them, turning the pages without hurry, keeping one eye on the court building. The car radio oozed wall-paper music as viscous as syrup but he didn't bother to change the station; it kept him company without calling attention to itself and he had distractions enough: he kept thinking of Irene.

He'd made a few unusual preparations. He'd smeared the car's license plates, front and back, with oil and dirt to render them unreadable. He'd bought a winter hat, a Russian sort of thing with earflaps; when pulled down tight it covered everything above his eyes and behind his ears. He'd bought an oversize pair of sunglasses—the mirrored ones, motorcycle goggle-style. And he'd pasted to his upper lip a bushy mustache from a theatrical supply shop. It had occurred to him that if he were to stalk them in daylight he must run the risk of being seen. That was all right but he wanted them to remember the hat, the goggles and the mustache.

The goggles and hat rested on the seat under the newspapers. The flat little .25 automatic was in his hip pocket; the .38 Centennial was clipped under the car seat where he could reach it fast.

A patrol car crunched past and stopped at the courthouse door. A cop and a man in a business suit escorted two youths from the cruiser into the building; the cop returned in a few moments and drove away. Paul looked at his watch: 9:45.

A number of people drifted into the building in the course of the next quarter hour. Paul watched them with distracted mild interest; his mind was on Irene. He kept picturing her laugh, the way her hips moved when she walked, the characteristic glint of secret amusement behind her long eyes.

She was the woman he would love if he could afford to love.

He watched people come and go; then around half past ten he saw two sullen boys emerge from the building and trail reluctantly after a very fat weary woman. Probably she was their mother: probably they had been released in her custody: they were small, likely no older than thirteen and fourteen, but they had the atavistic faces of children to whom brutality was the only reality.

The three of them waited on Ogden for the bus and when they boarded it Paul followed, switching the radio off, fitting hat and goggles to his head.

They transferred to a southbound bus on Ashland and he shadowed it into the ghetto; he was two blocks behind the bus when mother and boys left it and picked their way through the snow into a side street.

A small tenement absorbed them and Paul sat in the car for an hour waiting for the children to come out. But when they emerged they only joined three other boys and the five of them went along to a small park. One of the boys was dragging a sheet of hard green plastic with an upcurved end —a sled. They had snowball fights and dragged the sled to the top of a diminutive hill and pummeled one another for the right to ride it; in the end three piled on the sled and tobogganed crazily down the slope, the sled tipping, two of them flying free and sledding to the bottom on the rumps of their trousers.

Angry with himself for his misjudgment Paul put the car in gear and went away.

He lunched cheerlessly on a hamburger which only put him wishfully in mind of Irene: her cooking was unpretentious but he'd rediscovered the fact that the most important pleasure in a meal was the sharing of it.

By one o'clock he was back on station at the curb, posting watch on the Juvenile Court. He was here because he couldn't very well return to the adult Criminal Court; if

Paul visited that court again and his visit was followed by a vigilante incident involving a felon whom the court had turned loose on bail, Irene would see the connection.

If a fourteen-year-old committed rape and murder the worst punishment he could receive was eighteen months in a training school and that usually meant seven or eight months because they were turned loose early on account of the overcrowding in the institutions. Perhaps the leniency of the juvenile laws had been justified in the days when the laws had been written: children then had been merely children. But the children of the streets had degenerated to vile savagery. Juvenile dockets were heavy with mutilations and murders, rapes, brutal vandalizings of human beings. The only purpose the law served was to reassure them they could commit bestialities without fear of punishment.

The ones who'd attacked Esther and Carol had been young; no one knew exactly how young but they'd been boys, not men. The young ones were the worst: they hadn't learned inhibitions. He'd read somewhere that the chief reformer was age. You rarely found a forty-year-old mugger; as they matured they learned fear.

It was after two o'clock before he knew he had a strike on the line.

The kid was probably seventeen or eighteen. He parked his half-wrecked car behind Paul's by the fire hydrant and walked across the avenue kicking slush with his boots. He was tall and tight in a denim jacket and black chinos; he'd been wearing one of those insolent cowboy hats but he'd left it in the car. He made a show of not minding the cold.

He was too old to be a respondent here; he could only have come to pick someone up. Paul waited for him to reappear.

People came out of the building in little groups: parents and children, abraded by the machinery within, solemn and some of them alarmed by whatever had taken place inside the cold black building.

Paul had the engine running and the heater fan blowing hard when the tall kid in the denim jacket came out of the building with another boy dressed in almost identical costume; the second boy was smaller and younger but his features had the same apathetic cast. The two of them came across the street with their hands in their trouser pockets, not talking; their eyes were glossy and hooded—completely without expression: nothing more than eyes, sighted organs.

They got into the car behind him. He heard the doors rattle when they scraped shut. There was the growl of a rotted exhaust muffler and foul smoke erupted behind the ruined car; it swerved out past Paul and rutted forward on its shot springs to the corner.

He let it go out of sight around the corner before he began to stalk them.

The clanking old Mercury seemed to be moving in random directions at first: it turned corners, doubled back, wandered without purpose. Trying to disclose a tail? But he had no trouble staying with them. He remained a block or two behind them, allowing traffic to intervene; his own car was commonplace and anonymous, its paint a little faded, covered with the grey-black streakings of slush and road oil.

Probably they were deciding what to do: thinking up entertainment. He found himself hoping they'd decide to go to a movie. It surprised him but he had no desire for violence.

The Mercury ahead of him drew past the playground of a school. Paul slowed when he entered the intersection; he put his turn indicator on, flashing his intention to make a left. He'd decided to drop it: go back to the office, drop off the guns and the hat and goggles and mustache, go home and shower and shave and put on his tweed suit. He and Irene had been invited to dinner tonight by Harry Chisum, the old law professor.

He was halfway into the turn when he saw the Mercury pull over to the curb and stop.

It was at the far end of the playground on the street he'd just turned off. He stopped his car in the side street and watched through the mesh of the playground's high fence. The two kids in denim got out of their car and began to walk. Young children were flowing across the playground from the gradeschool building, carrying their books; their breath clouded the air around them. School had just been dismissed for the day: the children were on their way home.

The two thin boys in denim stood at the mesh fence with their gloved fingers hooked in the wire, watching the small children cross the playground.

They had something in mind. Something evil.

Paul put the car in gear. Rolling through the side street he slipped his hands into the rubber gloves; he put on the hat, turned left at the corner, put on the sunglasses and went on to the farther corner; and turned left again.

He'd gone around three sides of the block, behind the school, and now he drove slowly toward the front corner where the children were flowing through the gate onto the sidewalk. Ahead of him the two boys in denim had backed away from the fence and were walking toward the gate corner. They fell in behind a pair of nine-year-old girls and crossed the street while a fat woman in traffic warden uniform held the cars at bay.

When the woman blew her whistle to allow the traffic to proceed Paul crossed into the street beyond. The two youths were ahead of him, still walking with their hands in their pockets; the two little girls were ahead of them and skipped into a broad vacant lot where something had been torn down and a few dilapidated cars were parked askew: they were short-cutting home. The empty land extended straight through to the far side of the block. The two boys in denim stood on the sidewalk and watched the little girls cross the lot. As Paul drove past them the two boys turned and began to follow the girls.

Paul accelerated toward the far corner: he wanted to get around the block by the time the little girls reached the far side of it. While he drove through the narrow street he leaned across the car and rolled the right-hand window down; then he made the second right turn and slowed the car, reaching under the seat for the Centennial. Inside the rubber gloves his hands began to pucker in the confinement of sweat.

He pushed the lever into neutral and let the car roll forward silently; he was leaning forward, peering past the brick corner as the vacant lot came in sight.

The two denim-cased boys stood in the shadows. The little girls cowered against the bricks, cornered and terrified.

The tall boy—the driver—flicked his hand out as if snapping his fingers. But Paul saw the glint of the knife blade as it flipped open.

The younger boy moved forward, deliberately ominous, grinning with a sadistic show of teeth: dramatizing his brutality. He bent, reached for the hem of the larger girl's coat and yanked it upwards, holding the hem in his fist and pressing the girl back against the wall. She wore white socks halfway up her thighs and dusky white underwear. The boy reached for the elastic.

Paul steadied his aim. The boys were intent on their victims: they noticed nothing except the flesh beneath them. The boy with the knife moved closer to the smaller girl and held her throat with his free hand, pinioning her, choking off her attempt to scream. The other boy ripped the panties

143

off the older girl. He was still holding her coat and skirt bunched up against her chin.

Something made Paul lower the sights a fraction before he fired.

The first bullet took the younger boy in the back of the knee.

The Centennial leveled again across the car sill: Paul was leaning across the seat, firing through the open passenger window, his wrist balanced on the metal. The taller boy was turning, disoriented: the bullet had slammed his friend against him, upsetting his balance, and Paul shot him as he turned: the soft-nose punctured his calf and by the way the boy's leg twisted it was evident it had smashed the bones.

Both of them fell, broken-legged.

The little girls flattened themselves in terror against the brick; their round eyes swiveled toward Paul.

On the ground the taller boy crawled in a circle of pain like a half-crushed beetle. His partner seemed stuporous; his mouth hung slack and he hardly moved.

In a sudden burst the older girl grabbed the younger one by the elbow and dragged her away. An instant later they were both running in panic, back across the empty lot toward the farther street, leaving their schoolbooks abandoned in the snow.

Paul rolled up the window and straightened in the seat. He made a tight U-turn.

30

"CHILDRESS will eat you alive if you give him a chance," Harry Chisum said.

"I've been forewarned." Paul caught Irene's sudden smile. "Anyhow I'm sure it won't be boring."

"It's a dynamic firm," the old man agreed. "Well then. More coffee, everyone." He poured from a silver decanter; his aged hand shook a bit. The dining room was like the rest of the house: a relic. Probably nothing in it except the wiring had changed in fifty years. It was a frame house without pretension but it had been built in a time when there had been leisure for elegance of a kind; there was comfort in its solidity, in the heavy darkness of old woods and furniture built for relaxing.

Irene looked at her wrist watch. She'd checked the time frequently in the past quarter hour. "I'm not being rude, Harry, but I don't want to miss that program."

"You keep saying you want to see a program. I never knew you to be a television addict."

"It's the Cavender interview. He's going to be grilling Vic Mastro. I want to see what our famous cop has to say."

"What time does it begin?"

"Nine."

"Then there's plenty of time. Stop looking at your watch every half minute."

Around the house a frigid gale shook the windows. A wood fire burned on the hearth. Chisum measured out cognac and passed the goblets around; then he led the way into his parlor and seated Irene in an easy chair facing the television set. It was an antique console, a bulky block of walnut with a small screen set into it and a pair of tarnished rabbit ears perched on top.

Irene made a gesture toward Paul, lifting her glass an inch; he warmed to her private signals—he nodded and smiled before he tasted the brandy.

Chisum eased himself slowly into a wooden rocker. "How many did you have to turn loose this week?"

She was very dry: "It was a short week. We only inflicted half the usual dose on the public."

"Something's got your dander up, my dear."

"Gehler sentenced one of my prosecutions to a six-months suspended. The man's got an incredible record—he's been up the river as many times as an anxious salmon, and this was an open-and-shut burglary. Red handed. But Gehler let him off with an SS."

"It's one of the things we've got to do, isn't it?" Chisum said. "Take the discretionary power to set sentences out of the hands of the judges. It's no good having one judge who regards robberies by poor people as legitimate readjustments of economic inequities, while another judge treats every crime as a grave threat to the stability of the society. To

146

the one, any sentence is too heavy; to the other, most sentences are too light. How can we expect anything like 'equal justice for all' under those circumstances?"

The fire made a good smell. Paul relaxed on the leather couch: it was old leather, deep red gone almost black, the crow's-feet of age creased into it. An office couch—likely it had come out of the professor's law office when he'd retired. Chisum had run a vigorous criminal practice, he'd learned, before turning to writing and teaching. He'd been a prominent defense attorney for several years. Paul had been keenly surprised by that revelation. Now Chisum glanced at him and resumed the subject:

"You're still baffled, aren't you."

"I confess I am. You don't make noises like a civil libertarian."

"I'm not. I believe in discipline. It's the mortar that holds society together. Without discipline there's chaos." He smiled gently at Irene. "There was a time when this young lady thought me a fascist."

Paul said, "How do you reconcile that with your record as a criminal lawyer?"

"Easily. I believe that for all its grievous faults, there's no better juridical system than the adversary process where both sides are allowed to present their cases with the greatest vigor. There are dangers in it—chiefly the danger that the better of the two lawyers may win the case regardless of its justice—but in spite of those risks, I don't know of any system in all history that's proved better. If a fact is in dispute, you can only arrive at the truth by a vigorous examination of both sides of the story. That's what our system was designed to do, and when it works properly it's a splendid example of human achievement."

"When it works properly," Irene echoed, not without sarcasm.

"Every case brought before a criminal court deserves an intense prosecution," Chisum said. "But it also deserves the best possible defense. Defense attorneys, after all, are officers of the court, the same as prosecutors and judges. They're all components of one system, and the purpose of that system is to arrive at the truth of each case. If you don't have first-rate defense lawyers you may as well not have a trial at all."

"Forgive me if I'm impertinent," Paul said, "but that sounds to me a lot like the kind of rationalization you hear from big-time shysters when they try to explain away the fact that they're on some mobster's payroll."

"The argument's a valid one, no matter who uses it in his own defense," Chisum said. "It breaks down, of course, in cases where the mobster's lawyer is himself a member of the mob and a party to its illegal acts. That kind of syndicate mouthpiece is common enough, I'm afraid, but his existence shouldn't be used to try and discredit the whole fraternity."

The old man began to move back and forth in the rocker. "Adversary law is workable, we've proved that. The trouble today is that it doesn't apply in too many cases. The system to which we lawyers pledge our allegiance has become a shabby fiction. Most cases are decided by plea-bargaining, not by any genuine attempt to arrive at the truth. The guilty benefit while the innocent suffer, because a man who's truly innocent is less likely to be willing to plead guilty to a reduced charge, while a guilty man is eager to do so. No, the problem we have in our courts isn't the influence of defense lawyers. It's the wholesale breakdown of the adversary system. What we need is a restoration of the adversary process, not a further erosion of it."

"That means an enormous expansion of the system," Paul said. "You'd have to quadruple the number of courts and judges just to begin carrying the load. I'd like to see it happen, but who's going to pay for it?"

"We could afford it," Chisum said. "That's one of the points I'm trying to make in my book. Actually we'd save money, in the long run."

"How?"

"By reducing the cost society pays for crime. If we can restore our legal structure to the point where it makes the risks of criminal behavior much greater, we'll see a big reduction in crime. In the long run we should be able to reduce the size of the legal bureaucracy, but even before that happens we'll save enormous sums simply by the fact that fewer crimes will be committed and less money will be lost. Not to mention the reduction in human suffering. To build the legal and penal structure up to the necessary size will require a considerable initial outlay of money, but that expense will be recouped very quickly."

"Then what prevents us from doing it?"

"Politics, of course."

Irene shot bolt upright in her chair. "My program!" She rushed across to the console. "How do you turn this damn thing on?"

"The left-hand knob. No, the one below the screen on the left. . . ."

"I've got it."

"Your watch is fast, my dear. It's not nine yet."

Paul heard a faint high-pitched whistle; at first he thought his ears were ringing. A dot of light appeared in the center of the screen; it became a tiny picture which slowly expanded into a wavering grey image of a newscaster speaking into the camera, reading his lines off a TelePrompter above the lens. The image lacked stability and the center of the newsman's face kept slipping out to one side, distorting him like a funny-mirror in an amusement park. Gradually the sound system warmed up and the announcer's voice became audible in mid-sentence:

". . . up again for the month of November, according to figures released today in Washington. Wholesale prices increased another one and a half per cent, raising the index to thirteen percentage points above where it was a year ago at the same time. And finally, in local news, there was tragedy tonight in a West Side bakery when police responded to an alarm and found the owner and two saleswomen shot to death and a third saleswoman shot and wounded. According to the injured woman, who is listed in satisfactory condition in County Hospital, two armed men entered the bakery this afternoon and allegedly demanded all the money in the place. The owner of the bakery, Charles Liddell, allegedly drew a pistol from his belt and fired a shot at the intruders. The two robbers then allegedly opened fire at everything that moved, killing Liddell and two of his three employees, and injuring Mrs. Deborah Weinberg with two bullets in the hip and chest. The robbery suspects then fled on foot, and no money was taken. Mrs. Weinberg is reported as saying that Mr. Liddell had started carrying the pistol in his belt after hearing about the Chicago vigilante on radio news. And now, tonight's forecast calls for snow continuing into morning with possible accumulations of up to six inches. . . ."

Paul sat frozen in his seat staring at the screen. He felt prickles of sweat burst out on his forehead. When he looked down at the goblet in his hand he saw that his knuckles were white: he had all but crushed the glass.

To cover the shock he lifted the glass to his lips. His hand shook. He drank quickly and put the goblet down.

"And now stay tuned as Channel Eleven presents the Miles Cavender Interview. Mr. Cavender's guest tonight will be Chicago Police Captain Victor Mastro, chief of homicide detectives and commander of the special squad detailed to investigate the Chicago vigilante."

Paul looked around cautiously. Irene was watching the screen. He brought Chisum into focus. The old man looked away quickly, reaching for his cognac; but Paul was certain Chisum had been staring at him.

The program came on with a burst of electronic music and an announcement that the broadcast was made possible by a grant from an oil company. The moderator appeared on the screen, his face wavering from side to side as the weak tube groped for resolution; Paul leaned back, slid down on the couch until his head rested against its back; he forced himself to pay attention.

Mastro was a thin man with dark striking features. His glistening black hair was combed smoothly back over the small ears. He wore a police uniform with decorations on the blouse, although in the newspaper photos he'd been wearing civilian clothes. Mastro was smiling slightly as he listened to Miles Cavender's introduction; he didn't seem unnerved, there was no indication of stage fright.

". . . has been with the Chicago force for sixteen years, and before that was an officer with a Military Police detachment of the U.S. Army. He has received degrees in criminology and sociology from the University of Chicago, and was promoted to the rank of captain two years ago. There's talk around City Hall of a pending promotion for Victor Mastro to deputy superintendent. Do you have any comment to offer on that speculation, Captain?"

"I'd rather not. I've had no official indications from the department." Mastro's voice was smooth and confident, surprisingly deep for such a small man. He had an actor's resonance.

"One would assume," Cavender said with the insinuation

Ω BRIAN GARFIELD

of overprecise enunciation, "that such a promotion might be contingent on the outcome of the vigilante case. Is that possible, Captain?"

"Sure. We're like any organization—promotions come on the basis of incentives and performance."

"I appreciate your candor." Cavender had a slightly effeminate voice. He didn't leer but he was the prying sort of interviewer Paul disliked intensely: subtle courtesy masking hostility.

"Captain, we're here to talk about the vigilante. First, of course, there's the question that's been spoken a good many times lately. Is the vigilante real—or is the whole thing a myth that's been cooked up by City Hall in a desperate effort to stave off the continuing increase in the Chicago crime rate?"

Mastro's eyes flashed briefly but his answer was controlled and unhurried. "It's not a phony. We didn't create the vigilante. He's real, he's out there and he's using his guns. He shot two boys on the South Side this afternoon."

"What were the boys doing?"

"Apparently they may have been molesting two small girls who were on their way home from school."

" 'Apparently.' . . . 'May have been.' Aren't you sure?"

"We've talked to the little girls, and we've got the two boys in custody in the hospital."

"Then neither of them was killed by the vigilante. Isn't that a bit unusual?"

"These are the first victims who haven't been shot dead, yes."

"Can you account for it?"

"Not yet. It's possible he fired from a moving car. That may have thrown his aim off."

"How sure are you that this is the same so-called vigilante who's been blamed for the other killings?"

"The bullets appear to have come from the same revolver that was used in most of the other cases."

"You say 'most of the other cases.' Isn't it likely there are more than one of them?"

"Revolvers or vigilantes?"

Cavender smiled a bit. "Vigilantes, Captain."

"We know for sure that there is one vigilante. There may be a second one, but that hasn't been established beyond doubt."

"But the use in different cases of two admittedly distinct handguns . . ."

"He could own two guns, you know. Particularly today's case suggests that it's the same man. He used the thirty-eight revolver today, but he fired from his car, and that's the same pattern that's been established in two or three other cases where he's used the forty-five automatic."

"I see. Then you're pressing your investigation on the assumption that you're looking for a single culprit."

"We haven't closed any doors."

Cavender shifted in his chair; it was an indication he wanted to change to another angle of attack. "Captain, the *modus operandi* of the Chicago vigilante, whether one man or two men or an entire society of men, seems to be quite simple, in a sense. That is, he simply finds a criminal in the act of committing a crime, and shoots the criminal dead in his tracks. Would you agree that's a fair summary of his pattern?"

"It's what the evidence suggests."

"Yes. Well doesn't it seem curious to you that this vigilante seems to have very little trouble locating these people?"

"I'm not sure I understand your question."

"What I'm saying, Captain, is that the vigilante seems to find it very easy to find out who is going to commit a crime, and when and where the crime will take place. Then all the vigilante has to do is be at the right place at the right time. Now I suppose you must have devoted some part of your investigation to inquiring into that question, haven't you?"

"Naturally."

"The sources of the vigilante's intelligence, I mean. How he identifies the criminals. How he finds out when and where the crimes will take place." Cavender leaned forward now, peering at the policeman with something like a vindictive gleam. "How does he do it, Captain? How does he do it so easily?"

"There's a certain logic to it. In some of the cases it's pretty obvious that he sets himself up as a mark. He probably dresses fairly well, and a man who's well-dressed walking alone in some neighborhoods is an open invitation to a mugging. He just waits for them to come to him, and when they begin to attack him he kills them. It isn't that hard, if you know the city and the neighborhoods."

"I see. But what about the cases where he's interrupted crimes against other persons?"

"We have a theory that he has access to information about criminals. Possibly police records or court records. He finds the name and address of a criminal, we think, and then he stakes out the criminal and tails him until the criminal makes a move. Then the vigilante moves in for the kill. We're assuming this because nearly all his victims have had prior records of arrest and conviction. Therefore we assume the vigilante has access to these records. Of course a lot of them are matters of public record—he could find them in the official directories of court proceedings, or even the newspaper morgues."

"Yes. Or the files of the Police Department itself?"

"It's possible." Mastro actually smiled: it was evident he knew what was coming.

Cavender plunged. "Doesn't this suggest the strong possibility that the vigilante is himself a police officer?"

In the rocking chair Harry Chisum snorted. "What absolute bloody rubbish."

Mastro was still smiling, his grey face wavering on the television screen. "I wouldn't call it a strong possibility. But we admit it's a possibility. We're not ignoring that avenue of investigation. We're checking it out."

"Yes, of course. But it leads to a far more compelling question, doesn't it, Captain."

"What question?"

"Simply this. If the vigilante can so easily find these criminals, and beat them to the punch as it were, then *why can't the police do the same thing?*"

"You mean kill them on sight, Mr. Cavender?"

"You know perfectly well what I mean, Captain. Why can't our policemen be as successful as this vigilante in preventing crimes?"

"Actually they are. They're far more successful, as a matter of fact."

"You've just lost me, Captain."

"We assign plainclothes officers to shadow known criminals, particularly some of those who are let out on bail, or those who have just returned from prison, or others when we receive tips from our informants that they're planning something. We have a sizable group of detectives that's assigned to surveillance of these suspects, and quite often the surveillance results in arrests when the officers apprehend the suspects in the act of committing crimes. But the point is, these arrests don't generate the kind of publicity the vigilante gets with his cold-blooded murders. As a case in point, the vigilante has killed at least sixteen people in the past two weeks or so—or at least that's the number of killings that have been attributed to him. At the same time, our stakeouts have resulted in more than forty arrests, under very similar circumstances. But naturally these arrests don't make headlines the way vigilante murders do."

"An entire metropolitan police department prevents only two or three times as many crimes from being consummated as one man with a couple of handguns. Isn't that a pretty woeful batting average for the police?"

"We don't have unlimited funds or unlimited manpower, Mr. Cavender. If we had enough men and money to put tails on every suspected criminal in the streets of Chicago, we'd do it, believe me. It would make our job a whole lot simpler. But we've got a great deal to do, an enormous territory to cover, and a great many duties other than crime prevention and suspect-shadowing. We're spread thin, and I think we're doing a damn good job considering everything."

"I have no doubt you feel that way, Captain, but I think you can understand how some of us may not agree with you completely."

"That's your privilege."

"I'm impressed, at any rate, by the fact that you haven't chosen to rear back on your dignity and plead that you've been hamstrung by the laws about entrapment and such."

"We do have those problems, yes, but there's not much point bleating about them. We've got to operate within the system as it is, not as we'd like it to be."

"I think we're all fortunate that's the case, Captain. Very well, I'd like to get your views on another side of this subject. What can you tell us about the vigilante himself?"

"In what sense?"

"What sort of person is he? Have you formed an impression of him?"

"A physical description?"

"Well obviously we're all eager to know whether you have a description of the man yet, after all this time, but in addition to that, I think our audience is curious to know what picture of the vigilante you may have formed in your own mind. What sort of personality he is. What his character is. Anything you may have concluded about his background, or especially his motives. But let's start with the physical description, since you mentioned it. What does he look like?"

"I'd prefer not to go into much detail about how much we know about him. I can say this much. We believe he's a male Caucasian."

"A white man."

"Yes."

"Ruling out blacks, Spanish-Americans, Orientals, American Indians, women and children. Well that's quite a step, Captain, it must narrow the field right down to two or three million suspects."

Mastro only smiled in reply; he was, Paul saw, genuinely amused.

"What else can you tell us, then? Do you think he has delusions? That he suffers, for example, from messianic fantasies?"

"I'm not a psychiatrist. I don't know. All we have is the record of what he's actually done. He could have any number of motives or delusions."

"He's been clever enough to elude your massive task force for quite a long time now."

"He's not a raving maniac, no." Mastro was still smiling with the side of his mouth. "He's probably an ordinary citizen unless you happen to catch him with a smoking gun in his hand."

"Well obviously there's at least one important difference between the vigilante and the rest of us ordinary citizens."

"He shoots people."

"Yes, quite."

Mastro said, "I think everybody has fantasies of violence at one time or another. Even the most civilized people experience anger at some point in their lives. Your wife is mugged, or your kid is beaten up, or somebody slashes the tires of your car—the nature of the offense is almost beside the point. It's the sense that you personally have been violated. I remember once years ago I left my car parked on a side street while my wife and I visited some friends. It was our personal car, not an official vehicle. We had an old convertible at the time. When we left our friends' house and returned to our car, I found that the canvas roof had been slashed by vandals. Well it was an old clunker of a car, the whole car probably wasn't worth a hundred dollars, and no real lasting damage or great cost had been inflicted on me. But in spite of the fact that I've been a cop all my adult life and I've had to deal with things that are unspeakably worse than this trivial vandalism of a piece of canvas, I still had a predictable natural reaction to this event."

"What was it?"

"The same as yours or anybody's, under equivalent circumstances. For just a moment there, in the hot rage of the instant, I had the feeling that if I'd been there in time to see the man slash the car, I'd have killed the son of a bitch in his tracks."

"You would?"

"Instant gut reaction, Mr. Cavender. I'd been threatened. That car, poor as it was, was my own personal property, and by attacking it this guy had violated *me* in a very personal sense."

"Would you really have shot him if you'd caught him in the act? You do carry a gun."

"Yes, I carry a gun, and no, I would not have shot him. I've been a police officer for twenty-two years, including service with the military, and I've never killed a man with a gun."

"Never?"

"I've shot a few and wounded them but I've never killed a man."

"You must be rather proud of that record. I know I commend it."

"Thank you. I can't say it's always a matter of choice. Perhaps I've been lucky: I've never been pushed into a position where I had no choice but to kill, in the line of duty. I don't think we can condemn officers who've found themselves in the position, though."

"Let's get back to the slashing of your car."

"I carry a gun. If I'm not mistaken, I had it on my person that night when we discovered the vandalism. And my gut reaction, as I said, was red-hot anger: I'd have killed the guy, I told myself, if I'd caught him. Now the point is, I wouldn't actually have killed him. I'd have arrested him. But that situation didn't apply, you see. The guy wasn't really there—he'd done his slashing and he was long gone by then. And *because* he wasn't there, I was free to indulge in this angry fantasy of killing the guy in retaliation for his violation of my person. Do you see what I'm getting at?"

"You're saying nearly everybody has experienced that kind of fantasy at one time or another."

"Yes. It's a natural thing, it's a human reaction. A sort of safety valve. But fortunately most of us have inhibitions, we're conditioned by the rules of our society, we have consciences. We don't actually shoot people for minor infractions. But we do dream about it from time to time. The guy who insulted you in the parking lot last week—you dream about going back there and punching him in the face until he's a bloody wreck. But of course you don't actually do it. You wouldn't get any pleasure out of it even if you did. The pleasure is in the fantasy, because in fantasies you don't have to worry about conscience or inhibitions."

"Go on, Captain."

"All I'm saying is, the vigilante is like everybody else, except for one thing. Somewhere in him, there's a wire down. There's been a disruption of contact between fantasy and reality. The conscience and inhibitions have been neutralized by this breakdown, and he's free to go out and act out these fantasies which are perfectly natural in all of us, *but only so long as they remain fantasies.* The minute he begins to act these things out, he steps over the boundary between civilization and savagery, between conscience and amorality."

"Between, if you like, good and evil."

"Yes."

"Captain, I must admit you're an impressive man. You've got a good mind, you're far better spoken than I'd anticipated."

"We're not all lump-headed flatfeet, Mr. Cavender."

Cavender said, "Let me act as devil's advocate for a moment, Captain. It's been said, rather loudly and in conspicuous places, that the vigilante has been a force for good in this city. That his actions, and the publicity about them, have acted as a deterrent. That he's neutralized a few thugs and scared a lot more of them off the streets. Now we've heard a lot of statistics since this man started. We've heard that muggings are way down, and we've heard that they aren't. You've been remarkably candid with me tonight, and I wonder if I can impose on you to be equally candid in answering this one. Can I?"

"Well the statistics are down, that's a fact. They're down about twenty per cent in the past two weeks. Part of that is the seasonal drop—the Christmas spirit and all that. Part of it's probably attributable to the vigilante, but there's no way to put a specific figure on it."

"That's honest enough."

"I can tell you this much. It's not an enormous drop. I mean he hasn't scared half the crooks off the streets or anything like that. He may have dissuaded ten per cent of them—temporarily."

"Well that means one mugging in ten hasn't taken place, doesn't it?"

"You could put it that way," Mastro said in even tones. "But I'd like your audience to see it this way also. This afternoon a bakery owner who said he'd been inspired by the vigilante tried to shoot it out with two bandits in his bakery. He ended up dead, and he ended up getting all three of the shop assistants shot along with him. Two of them died and the third one was badly wounded. And a few days ago we had a bus driver shoot an unarmed man to death. The bus driver was another fan of the vigilante's. I think we're going to see a lot more tragedies like those before this thing is finished, and I'd like to ask people to just think about it before they arm themselves and go out into the streets looking for trouble. What's more important, a few wallets and handbags and television sets, or the lives of innocent people and unarmed people?"

"I certainly agree with that wholeheartedly, Captain."

"Violence answers no questions," Mastro said. "But unfortunately it's a spreading infection. It's a lot harder to stop it than it is to start it."

"Yes. Well thank you very much, Captain." Cavender turned to the camera. "We've been talking with Captain Victor Mastro of the Chicago Police Department," he began, and Irene switched the set off. The picture dwindled to a piercing white dot that whistled for a while before it died.

Harry Chisum said, "He's fighting a losing battle."

Paul looked at him, trying to ascertain his tone.

Irene said, "Cavender, or Vic Mastro?"

"Your good captain," Chisum said. "I don't think he'll ever find his vigilante."

"Don't you? You may be underestimating him. He's a good cop. One of the best."

"I'm sure he is. I was very impressed. So were a lot of other people watching, I'm sure. One gets the feeling Captain Mastro has just throw his hat into the political ring."

"I've had that feeling for a week or more," Irene agreed. "But why won't he catch the vigilante, Harry?"

"I can think of two reasons. One is that it would be an embarrassment to Mastro, in the long term. He'd lose more votes than he'd gain."

"Assuming he really does have the ambitions we're imputing to him."

"Yes, assuming that."

"And the other?"

"I think the vigilante has run his course," Harry Chisum said. He glanced at Paul and went back to Irene: "He's done what he set out to do. It's beginning to backfire on him now. It's beginning to have unpleasant consequences that he didn't anticipate when he started. I think, to use the vernacular, that pretty soon the vigilante is going to hang up his guns."

Irene laughed. "Sometimes you get downright fanciful, Harry."

"Don't you think I'm right?"

"No. I think the man's got the smell of smoke and the taste of blood in him now. I think he's gone rogue. I don't believe anything will stop him short of handcuffs and a prison cell—or a bullet."

"Care to place a small wager on it?" The old man was smiling.

"Are you serious?"

"Certainly. What would you say to fifty dollars?"

"Why Harry, gambling is illegal."

"Weaseling out? No courage with your convictions?"

"I'll take the bet." She grinned at him.

Harry Chisum turned his head. Paul couldn't make out his expression; the light was behind the old man. "What about you, Paul?"

"I'll pass. I'm afraid I haven't got a side to pick."

"If you change your mind let me know. I'm always glad to take a sucker's money."

"Harry's a fanatical bridge player," Irene said.

And probably pretty good at poker too, Paul thought. He wished he could fathom what was transpiring behind those dewlappy eyes.

They talked for another hour before the old man saw them to the door. He was all affability when he shook Paul's hand and urged him to come again. When the door closed Paul thought he glimpsed something else in Chisum's face: a hint of reproach—or did he imagine it?

Driving Irene back to the city he hardly spoke at all.

Ω

31

¶ CHICAGO, JAN. 5TH—Last night, for the second time in little more than 24 hours, Chicago's vigilante struck again, killing one man and injuring two others.

The dead man apparently was an innocent bystander, the intended victim of a robbery allegedly committed by the two wounded men.

Two men who allegedly had been rolling drunks near several bars in the Loop were found by police officers on Wabash Avenue shortly after 1:00 a.m. this morning, bleeding from .45 caliber bullet wounds, while a third man lay dead nearby.

According to Sergeant James Anderson of the Central District Patrol, the dead man has been identified as Peter A. Whitmore, 43, of 4122 Albion in Lincolnwood. Apparently Whitmore was on his way from a Balbo Avenue bar to the Harrison Street El station, on foot, when he was accosted on Wabash Avenue by the two alleged robbers, whose identities have been withheld by police pending further investigation. The two men allegedly knocked Whitmore down and were going through his pockets when they were fired on from a passing car.

One of the men was shot in the shoulder, the other wounded twice, in the hip and in the collarbone. The bullet which passed through the second man's hip barely grazed the flesh, according to police, and it continued on its trajectory, killing Whitmore almost instantly when it struck him in the temple.

According to Sergeant Anderson, the two men said the car from which the shots were fired never stopped moving, and they did not see the gunman's face or note the type or license number of the car.

Captain Victor Mastro, charged with investigating the series of vigilante shootings, said last night in a telephone interview from his home that ballistics analysis on the bullets recovered from the dead and wounded man had not yet been completed. "But we're proceeding on the assumption they were fired from the same .45 caliber automatic pistol that's been used in several other vigilante cases."

At a press conference yesterday afternoon, Captain Mastro revealed for the first time the specific descriptions of the two known handguns that have been identified by ballistics studies as having been used in the so-called Vigilante killings. One has been identified as a .45 Luger automatic, Captain Mastro said, and the other has been identified as a .38 S&W Centennial revolver. Laboratory study of the bullets recovered in several cases led to these identifications, according to Captain Mastro.

Such identifications are made possible by the fact

that each different firearm model possesses a distinctly machined bore. When a bullet fired from the weapon passed through the barrel, the "lands and grooves" of rifling that have been machined into the steel, in order to spin the bullet, leave their imprint on the bullets. Microscopic examination of fired bullets can provide, in most cases, the exact make and model of the weapon from which they were fired. Later, of course, if a weapon is recovered by police, a sample bullet can be fired from it and compared with those used in earlier shootings, to determine whether the specific handgun in possession was used to fire the earlier bullets. Such ballistics identifications are as positive and exact as fingerprint identification, according to Captain Mastro; no two handguns will leave exactly the same markings on a bullet fired from them.

The two wounded men in last night's shooting are being held in custody in the jail wing of County Hospital, according to a Central District spokesman. They are being questioned further about the incident.

Last night's shootings bring to twenty-one the toll attributed to the vigilante. Of those, only four have survived their injuries. The death last night of Peter Whitmore marks the first time an innocent bystander has been shot by the vigilante, according to police. "Apparently he didn't intend to shoot Whitmore," Sergeant Anderson said. "He was shooting from a moving car, as far as we can tell, and his aim may have been disturbed by hitting a bump or something."

"You could call it an accident," Captain Mastro agreed in the telephone interview last night, "but according to law it's first-degree murder. The felony-murder statute specifies that any homicide committed during the commission of another felony—in this case the assault against the two alleged robbers—is automatically classified as first-degree murder, even if the homicide took place accidentally."

In any case, Captain Mastro remarked, "He's got enough scores against him so that when we catch him we won't have to worry very much about the technicalities of this particular homicide. He's got a lot more than that to answer for. But this type of so-called 'accident,' involving the violent death of an innocent party, is all too typical of what happens when vigilantism rears its head."

32

SHE WAS ASLEEP with one hand clutched in her hair. He eased out of the bed and padded into the bathroom. The tiles struck cold under his feet. He shut the door before he switched on the light. Washed and used her toothbrush and had a look at his Sunday-morning eyes in the medicine cabinet mirror. Things were breaking up: it was harder to keep a grip on them. In the mirror he was drawn, grey, blear; he felt jumpy.

He switched it off and went back into the bedroom. A little morning greyness filtered in through the closed slats of the blinds; he found his clothes and picked them up and carried them silently out to the living room, and shut the door behind him before he dressed. Laced up his shoes, got his coat from the hall closet and let himself out of her apartment.

He had trouble starting the car and when he put it in

gear it stalled. He cursed aloud and finally willed it, chugging and bucking, into the street.

She'd wake up in an hour or two and she'd phone him to find out why he'd sneaked out before breakfast. He'd have to have an answer ready. He worked it out while he drove.

It was warmer than it had been in weeks and the pavements were going to slush. Passing cars threw up great filthy wakes around them like yachts at high speed. The sun was shining, a thin pale disc above the haze, but he had to keep the wipers on.

He put it in its garage slot and took the elevator up to the lobby, getting off there because he wanted to pick up yesterday's mail; he hadn't been home since Friday. He crossed to the mail room and put his key in the box. Bills and bulk-mail ads; nothing interesting; he dropped the ads in the trash bin and went back toward the elevators and that was when he saw the old man rising from the chair.

He was stunned. He stopped in his tracks.

"Good morning, Paul." Harry Chisum was affable enough.

"How long have you been here?"

"Half an hour perhaps. I came by yesterday but you weren't here."

"Irene and I were doing the art museums."

"Yes well I suspected you two were together. I didn't want to trouble Irene with it. I wanted an opportunity to talk to you alone." Chisum had a deerstalker and a walking stick in his hand; he wore a tweed jacket with leather patches on the elbows, and a bulky grey cashmere sweater under it; he looked younger than Paul had seen him before but his expression was grave.

"You could have phoned, saved yourself all that traveling back and forth." Paul heard the ring of his own voice and resented it: it sounded hollow.

"It's better this way. I didn't want to—forewarn you."

"Very mysterious."

"Am I? Well why don't we go up to your apartment."

"Yes of course. I'm sorry. . . ."

In the elevator he touched his thumb to the depressed plastic square and watched it light up. The old man tucked the walking stick under his arm. It was a slender stick of hardwood, gone completely black with antiquity; it had a head that appeared to be a chunk of ivory fixed to the stick with a bronze collar. It didn't mesh with Chisum's tweed and cashmere; it was the sort of thing you carried when you wore an opera cape. But the old man was indifferent to appearances.

"Well then, to what do I owe this honor?" It sounded weak and silly; he immediately regretted having uttered it.

"I think you know." Chisum's words had a dry rustle. The doors slid open; Paul led the way along the corridor, fumbling for keys.

He let the old man waddle in ahead of him; he shot the locks before he pocketed the keys and shrugged out of his coat. "I haven't had breakfast yet. Join me?"

"Just coffee. I've eaten." Chisum trailed him toward the kitchen and stood there with one shoulder propped against the jamb. He unbuttoned the jacket and let it hang back; his flannel trousers were pleated and cinched high and looked more than ever like a mailbag.

Paul busied himself with utensils. His hands rattled things. He tried to concentrate on it, to avoid looking at the old man. The silence became almost unbearable: finally he wheeled. "All right. What is it?"

"She's dented your armor, hasn't she. It's taught you to be afraid, and that's no good. Fear must be avoided like a whore with gonorrhea."

"What are you talking about?" The pulse was thudding in his temples.

"Friday evening—that news report about the baker and his saleswomen. I was watching your face, Paul. I think that was the moment when the enormity of your error struck you fully for the first time. If I hadn't been looking right at you at that moment I suppose I'd never have suspected. But the whole thing was written on your face. You're not a very good actor—you're a poor dissembler, really, I'm amazed you've been able to keep the secret this long."

"I'm trying to be polite, Harry, but I'm getting a little impatient. I have the feeling I've just wandered into a one-act drama of the absurd by mistake."

"There's an old Japanese proverb: You can see another's ass but not your own. But I think things started to fall apart for you the other night—or perhaps even earlier. You've been discovering yourself all over again, haven't you. Irene has exposed things in your heart you'd forgotten existed. You could only prevail so long as you could convince yourself that no point of view other than that of your own prejudice existed. Your view of things took the form of a violent solipsism, and you had become the most dangerous of men—a man with an obsession. But there was no room in that structure for a relationship with any other human being. You were only safe as long as you could endure the fact that there was no one you wanted to confide in. You met Irene, and everything changed. The other day—those two boys at the playground, molesting the little girls. You couldn't kill them, could you. You shot them, you've lamed one of them for life, but you couldn't take their lives."

"Now wait just a minute. . . ."

"You're the vigilante. I have no doubt of it."

"You're crazy. Stark raving—"

"Stop it, you're wasting wind. Even if I were wrong it wouldn't hurt you to listen to what I have to say. And if I'm right it may save your life."

"What the *hell* are you talking about?"

Chisum shifted his stance: he leaned on the opposite side of the doorway. "The water's boiling."

The blood had drained from his head and a red haze clouded his view: he was afraid to move because he wasn't sure he wouldn't fall down.

The old man said, "The day you first met Irene at the criminal courthouse a man was released on bail from that very courtroom. A few hours later he was dead, shot by the vigilante. I'd known that all the time, but I only made the connection when I saw your face the other night after that news report. I'm not sure I can explain it more clearly than that. I simply knew, I saw it in your face—all of it."

"You're a lawyer. That's hardly evidence. You're barking up the wrong—"

"I'm not trying to pin anything on you. I'm not trying to trap you. But you may as well abandon these unconvincing protestations of innocence."

"Why haven't you gone to the police with these demented suspicions?"

"I have no intention of going to the police. That's what I want to talk to you about."

"If I'm the homicidal maniac you claim I am, you're running a tremendous risk. Didn't you think about that before you came here? If I've killed fifteen or twenty people what's to prevent me from killing you?"

"You've persuaded yourself that there's an important difference between you and your victims. You've never shot anyone who wasn't guilty, in your view, of a terrible crime. I haven't committed any crimes. Therefore you couldn't possibly kill me and justify it to yourself."

"You've got pat answers, haven't you." He was bitter. "You're the most incredible character I've ever met. I don't know whether to laugh or feel sorry for you." He felt stronger now but dulled, as if drugged: reality seemed to have receded to a point beyond arm's length. He spooned instant coffee into two mugs and stirred the water in. "How do you take it?"

"Black," Chisum said. "Just black, I'm in mourning— for that baker and his saleswomen, among others." He reached for the mug and backed away through the doorway. "Why don't we sit down?"

There was little choice but to follow him into the living room. Harry settled back on the couch carefully, balancing his coffee. Paul stood above him, watching with narrowed eyes.

"It is possible," the old man intoned, "that God's justice ordains that certain persons must die for the good of humanity. It's possible, but the fallible human conception of justice is probably inadequate to decide who is to die and who is to survive. To put it another way, Alexis de Tocqueville observed that it was the great privilage of the American system that citizens were permitted to make retrievable mistakes. Clearly a man who's been shot to death has no opportunity to retrieve his mistakes."

"Do you want to trade quotations, Harry? I'll give you Edmund Burke: 'Wars are just to those to whom they are necessary.' "

"To kill a man because it's 'necessary' isn't the same thing as killing a man because it's right. But you don't make that distinction, do you. You've been obsessed with the idea of your own personal brand of star-chamber justice, where you alone are judge and jury." Then Harry said overcasually, "At least you're no longer pleading ignorance. I may take your remark as an indication that I'm correct in my conclusion?"

"It's a wild guess, not a conclusion."

The old man gave a gloomy sigh.

Then Paul said quietly, "To be willing to die, so that justice and honor may live—who said that, Harry?"

"Don Quixote, I believe. Are you indicating your willingness to die in the service of your cause?"

"Well your vigilante would certainly have to feel that way, wouldn't he." Paul carried his coffee to the dinette table and drew out a chair. When he sat down the envelopes in his inside jacket scraped his chest and he withdrew them and dropped them on the table. He found himself worrying about them: How much did they amount to? They were the kind of trivialities with which the mind protected itself in great stress; he recognized that. The old man was talking and he tried to focus on it but for a little while Harry's words broke up in his mind and he only sat staring at the unopened envelopes.

"You began to see the enormity of it," Harry was saying. "The bus driver, the baker and his saleswomen, the others who will surely follow—people who give up their lives because they've been 'inspired' by your example. In your single-handed way you've done a remarkable job of calling forth the night riders, Paul."

Paul turned in the chair and watched him. Harry was leaning forward on his walking stick, both hands clasped over the knob, chin almost resting on hands. "After Irene it began to collapse for you. You must have been asking yourself, 'What kind of a monster am I?' You've begun to see how extremes can create and feed upon each other. You've been educating yourself, slowly, in what Victor Mastro and a great many others already know: vigilantes don't solve any problems—they only create new ones."

"Am I supposed to be impressed by your rhetoric? I'm tired. What's the bottom line?"

"It's time you quit. You tried an experiment, it didn't work out—you found a drug that cures the disease but kills the patient. Too many side effects. You didn't know that before, but you know it now. If you keep going, more innocent people will suffer. Things inside you will compel you to make mistakes until they find you and put you away; or you'll get killed by one of your intended victims, the way it almost happened with that man with the machete, because you'll get careless out of a subconscious need for punishment."

"That's ten-cent Freudianism."

"It will be agony for you to live with your conscience either way. But if you give it up immediately, at least you'll know you tried to correct your mistake as soon as you discovered it."

The old man stood up, putting his weight on the walking stick as he rose. "I'm not telling you anything you haven't told yourself. But it may help to have had me put it into words for you."

Paul looked aimlessly away. He felt a forlorn emptiness. Harry wasn't finished. "Vigilantism isn't the only thing you're going to have to give up."

"No?"

"I'm talking about Irene."

Rage pushed him out of the chair. "I've had about enough. . . ." But his voice trailed off and the anger flowed out of him as if a drainplug had been pulled. He only stood and brooded at the old man.

"You'd never be able to tell her. It would build a wall between you. Every time she said something that reminded you of it, even remotely, it would drive you farther apart. You see how it has to end."

175

"Good Christ," he whispered.

"Consider it part of your penance."

"Don't be glib with me."

"I'm not trying to patronize you, Paul. But there's something in the ancient concept of justice. We usually end up making some kind of payment for our transgressions. It's not a metaphysical thing, it's something basic in nature—the balance of opposites, what the Orientals call yin and yang. You're going to suffer, whatever happens. You may as well accept that. And there isn't much point in forcing Irene to suffer with you."

He couldn't stand still. He shuffled to the window and drew the blinds; he stared without seeing and then he turned toward the old man. "You made a bet with Irene that the vigilante would retire."

"Yes."

"Now you're trying to win your fifty dollars."

"I always hate to lose a bet." Harry picked up his deerstalker. "It's on Irene's account I came. I'm rather fond of her in my spinsterly fashion. I wanted to spare her some of the anguish, if I could."

Harry smiled, surprisingly gentle. "Also, of course, I wanted to confirm my deductions."

"And you think you have."

"I know I have."

"Then why not turn me in?"

"I gave it a good deal of thought."

"And?"

"She's told me what happened to your wife and daughter."

"What's that got to do with not turning me in?"

"If the same thing had happened to my wife and my daughter, I can't be absolutely certain I wouldn't have reacted the same way."

"Is that sufficient grounds for you to withhold knowledge of a crime?"

"I'm breaking no law. You've admitted nothing to me in so many words. I've withheld no evidence—only the conclusions I've reached from observation."

"You're splitting hairs, aren't you?"

"Are you trying to persuade me to turn you in?"

"I only want to be sure where you stand."

"You're in no danger from me. Not in the sense you mean."

"In what sense, then?"

"If you go on killing you'll destroy yourself. That's the danger. You'll destroy an incalculable number of innocent lives as well."

"They're destroyed every day by those animals in the streets."

"Ah, yes, but that's not the same thing—those aren't *your* crimes."

"They are if I stand by and let them happen."

"Edmund Burke again, yes? 'The only thing necessary for the triumph of evil is that good men do nothing.' But Burke didn't counsel people to commit murder, did he."

Harry moved walrus-like to the door. He couldn't get it open; Paul had to snap the locks for him. It brought him within a handbreadth of the old man. Harry's eyes were kind. "I'm sorry, Paul."

Then he was gone.

Paul shut the door and bolted the locks.

33

You play the cards you've been dealt.

He sat motionless, bolt upright, not stirring and not reckoning the passage of time.

The telephone.

It drove him to his feet in panic and alarm. He stared at the instrument while it rang. It went on ringing; he didn't move.

It would be Irene. He couldn't talk to her now. He waited, wincing. It rang an incalculable number of times before she gave up.

Afterward the silence was terrifying.

Ω

34

HE PUT HIS CAR in the spiral-ramp garage. It was nearly empty; the Loop was deserted on a Sunday; he walked to the shabby building and climbed the stairs, focusing on the chipped linoleum. Let himself into the office and sat behind the desk with his fist knotted. His face turned toward the filing cabinet where the guns were.

He had to think. It was imperative. But a paralyzing numbness had set in and he kept flashing on moments of terror that jumbled in his mind like falling bricks: bloody machete looming above him, striking forward; gunsights leveling on the purse-snatcher while the old Jew moved into range; staring eyes of the blind girl.

And Harry Chisum, his voice as mild and dry as wind through autumn leaves: *You're the vigilante.*

He was drawn to the cabinet. He slid the drawer open and stared down at the guns. Dull gleam of machined metal: silent motionless things squatting in the shadows of the drawer like deadly twin embryos.

He smote the drawer with his shoe, slamming it shut with terrible force. Within, the guns skidded across the thin metal and crashed against the back of the drawer, making it ring like a crashing car.

On a desperate impulse he lunged for the telephone but the receiver was dead: they hadn't connected it yet. He slammed it down.

Then reason pried up a corner of his desperation. He got out his handkerchief and scrubbed the telephone frantically. What else had he touched? He couldn't remember. He scraped the handkerchief along the arms of the chair, the top of the desk, the knobs on both sides of the door. He looked around.

The filing cabinet. He wiped down the drawer and its handle. Had he touched the guns with his bare fingers?

No; he'd only stared at them. He went to his coat and got out the rubber gloves and put them on.

He sank back in the chair, drained. He had to think.

The sun began to filter through the sooty windows. He watched the line between light and shadow. Imperceptibly it fanned across the floor, approaching the desk.

His mind was running very fast like a runaway engine that had burned out its brakes. Words and images clashed kaleidoscopically without connection or transition. He felt helpless—a chip in a hurricane. It debilitated his body: he had the feeling he couldn't rise from the chair. Sensations of drowning.

The sun moved toward him: a guillotine blade. It reached the leg of the desk and crawled up the side.

You could only prevail so long as you could convince yourself that no point of view other than that of your own prejudice existed. Your view of things took the form of a violent solipsism, and you had become the most dangerous of men—a man with an obsession. . . .

You must have been asking yourself, "What kind of monster am I?"

Things inside you will compel you to make mistakes. . . .

You see how it has to end.

The sun lapped over a corner of the desk top. Driven back by it, Paul struggled out of the chair.

He wrenched the door open and went out. It clicked shut behind him but he didn't bother locking it. He went down the two flights, pausing only to wipe the knobs of the outside door; when he was in the car on Grand Avenue he stripped off the rubber gloves and crumpled them in his pocket.

In his apartment he looked at the clock. It was after three. He stood in the center of the room taking deep breaths; dropped his coat on the couch and walked to the telephone.

"Paul—I was so worried."

"I'm sorry. Something came up. . . ."

"I'm sitting here throwing corks for the cat and trying not to think about cigarettes. Wherever did you rush off to? Are you all right?"

"I've got strange things going on in my mind."

"What?"

"I don't know. It's hard to put into words. Do you ever get so knotted up you want to scream?"

She said, "Anxiety. Poor darling. It passes, you know. Everybody tends to be depressed on Sunday afternoons."

"It's more than that. Look, this is a bitch of a thing to say, but I've got to be by myself for a while, try to sort these things out."

Her silence argued with him.

"Irene?"

"I'm here." She was hurt.

"I just don't want to tangle you up in my stupid neurotic problems."

"Please, Paul, can't—"

"I woke up this morning in a sweat," he lied desperately. "I thought you were Esther. It was incredibly vivid. Do you understand now?"

He could hear her breathing. Finally she said, "All right, Paul. I guess there's nothing much to say, is there."

"I'm sorry."

"I know."

His hand crushed the receiver against the side of his face. Her voice became distant: "Call me sometime, Paul."

"Take care. . . ."

"Yes, you too."

He cradled the phone very gently. And then he wept.

Ω

35

IT WENT DARK but he didn't rise to switch on the lights: he continued to sit passively with his hands folded on the table.

All of a sudden he had a desperate need for company. He couldn't stand the aloneness. He thought of going out —a bar. Perhaps that bar where he'd met the journalists.

He had his coat and was out the door before he stopped himself. He went back inside, hung up the coat and locked the door. Going to a bar was the last thing he could afford to do. The shape he was in, there was no telling what he'd let drop after he had alcohol inside him.

Out of the same need for companionship he switched on the television. He looked at the last ten minutes of a game show and laughed at the comedians' jokes. He looked at half an hour of African wild animal footage narrated by a washed-up television actor. He looked at five minutes of a situation comedy rerun and suddenly he was starving.

There wasn't much in the refrigerator. He made a meal

of odds and ends. He hadn't eaten anything since the night before; he consumed great mouthfuls with the plate balanced on his knees, sitting before the flickering television.

He watched a floor-wax commercial intently as if to memorize every line and camera cut; afterward he carried his empty dish to the kitchen and left it in the sink without stopping to rinse it. He poured three fingers of scotch into a tumbler and went back to the living room to drink it.

Station break: a car dealer offering five-hundred-dollar rebates on new compact cars; a furniture store that was fighting inflation; a supermarket chain marking down specials on turkeys and pot roasts; a shampoo that cleansed while it brightened; sixty great hits of the rock-and-roll years on four stereo albums for only seven ninety-nine. Call this number before midnight. Now here's tonight's news.

"At the top of the news tonight once again it's the vigilante. Two more men were shot in Chicago streets less than three hours ago. We take you now to Roger Bond, on the scene."

A reporter in a wind-blown trench coat faced the camera under portable floodlights. Behind him flurries blustered in a dreary street; two or three curious passers-by watched him in the background. There was nothing to be seen but the street and the reporter.

"On this King Boulevard sidewalk just a few hours ago another tragedy was acted out by Chicago's infamous vigilante and his victims. The police say the young man and the teen-age boy were making a connection here. The sale of four caps of heroin was going down when a forty-five caliber pistol roared four times in the quiet grey afternoon. It left the pusher and the addict dead together, their bodies sprawled across one another. We found Captain Victor Mastro at the mayor's fifth-floor office at City Hall. . . ."

The image cut to a corridor crowded with lights and

cameras and reporters. The same reporter in the same trench coat was thrusting his microphone under Mastro's face. There was a babble of voices, everybody asking questions at once.

"We haven't had a chance to check out ballistics yet," Mastro was saying. "But it looks like the same forty-five Luger from the other cases. We've got a witness who said the shots were fired from a car. . . . No, it was stopped, it pulled over and stopped before he did the shooting. It wasn't moving. . . . What? I can't hear you, I'm sorry. . . . Yes, this makes twenty-three all told. Nineteen dead. Eleven with the thirty-eight and twelve with the forty-five. . . . I'd rather not comment on what the witness saw, beyond what I've already told you. We're still interviewing him. . . . Intensifying it? No, we're not intensifying it. It's already as intense as it can get. We've got sixty officers assigned to this case alone, full time. What? . . . No, I can't describe the leads we're working on at this time. We do have leads, that's all I can say, and we're subjecting every one of them to an exhaustive and thorough examination. . . . I'm sorry, gentlemen, that's all for now."

The camera followed Mastro's back as he pried his way through the mob; then it cut to the studio moderator.

Paul switched it off. He crossed to the window and looked out at the lights. A haze brought the sky down low and brightened the city like a stage set.

It was a slim chance, it probably wouldn't lead to anything. But he had to do it. He had to try.

He went to the phone and searched for Spalter's home number; he'd written it down somewhere. . . .

Spalter came on the line, cheerful and ebullient. "Hey, Paul, How're they hanging?"

"Jim, something's come up. A personal thing, nothing vital, but I'm going to have to be out of town for a couple of days. I won't be able to start work until the middle of the week. I realize it's awkward but can you explain it to Childress for me? I'll report in on Wednesday or Thursday at the latest."

"You have to go back to New York?"

"Yes. It's a family thing. My wife's estate—you know these idiotic legal hassles. But it's got to be straightened out before it gets any worse."

"Sure, I know. Okay, Paul, I'll cover for you with the old man. Hope everything works out okay. I'll see you Wednesday or so, right?"

"Thanks very much."

"Don't mention it, buddy. Have a good trip—give my love to Fun City."

He rang off and reached for his drink. It was probably a bad hunch. The thing probably was still squatting there under the glass countertop, untouched since he'd seen it weeks ago. But there was a chance. He had to find out.

36

HE WAS OUT and rolling before the Monday morning rush. By seven he was crossing the Wisconsin line. A little while later he left the divided highway and switched off the headlights. Snow lay in deep drifts on the verges: the countryside looked like something in a calendar photograph, sunlight on rolling fields of snow, the occasional farmhouse on a far hilltop. The world was new and clean.

The shop hadn't opened yet and he sat in the car until restlessness prohibited it; then he walked through town and back while the cold stung his ears and came inside his coat. From a block away he saw Truett limp to the door and unlock the security gate and roll it up. Truett unlocked two or three bolts and perhaps a burglar alarm and finally went inside; two minutes later Paul entered the cluttered shop.

"Morning."

"Hello there. Mr. Neuser, isn't it?"

"You've got a good memory."

"Pride myself," Truett said. His moist eyes peered up at Paul and then he continued on his rounds, switching lights on. "What can I do you for?"

He'd thought of half a dozen lies during the night and rejected them; finally he'd settled on the simplest story and rehearsed it until it was smooth. "I was talking to my brother-in-law about my last visit up here. I mentioned that Luger I saw in your collection. The forty-five. He got very interested—he's a gun buff and he served in Germany with the Occupation after the war. Anyway it's his birthday coming up and I wondered if you still had the thing for sale. I don't see it here under the counter."

"Sold that one a few weeks ago. Just a few days after you were here, matter of fact." Truett still had the folded newspaper under his arm; now he limped around behind the counter and put the newspaper down before he reached up to pull the switch-strings of the ceiling fluorescents.

It was a Milwaukee newspaper. That relieved Paul. If Truett didn't get the Chicago papers he probably wasn't aware of the ballistics reports; details that small wouldn't be printed in Milwaukee papers or reported on Milwaukee television, he was sure.

"That's too bad," Paul said, trying to keep his feelings out of his voice. "It'd make such an ideal birthday present for Jerry."

"I sure am sorry, Mr. Neuser. Maybe there's something else I might turn up. Got a nice World War Two Walther in the back room, practically mint condition, the old double-action P-thirty-eight model. . . ."

"No, Jerry really got excited over that forty-five Luger. Say, I'll tell you what, Mr. Truett. Maybe the fellow who bought it from you wouldn't mind turning a quick profit on it."

"Well. . . ."

Paul opened his wallet and counted out bills. "Of course you'd be entitled to a finder's fee and a commission." He spread the fifty dollars on the glass. "Do you happen to have the name and address of the fellow you sold it to?"

"Well sure I do. Have to take down all that stuff for the Federal registration, don't I."

Ω
_____

37

IT WAS a small house on Reba Place in Evanston, in the middle of a block of elderly detached houses on postage-stamp lots, each driveway forming the boundary with its neighbor's property; the houses were narrow and old-fashioned and the trees along the curbs had attained towering heights. The carport alongside the house had no cars in it. Paul didn't go up to the door but he sensed the house was empty.

He had a name—Orson Pyne—and this address. He sat in his car and studied the house and tried to form a picture of the man who lived in it. He had little success. But he had a strong feeling the house was empty and that meant either Pyne lived alone or his wife worked. The place wasn't equipped for two cars but that didn't mean much; it was only two or three blocks' walk to Asbury where you could pick up a Western Avenue bus.

190

There was a filling station on the corner two and a half blocks away. It was worth a try. Before he started the car Paul opened his wallet and sorted through the ID's and business cards. There was a lot of outdated junk, he saw —even a 1973 plastic calendar—and he was amazed it had been that long since he'd gone through the contents of the wallet. He decided on the card that identified him as a member of the West 71st Street Community Association. It had been sent to him when he'd made a financial contribution to the block association's campaign to install high-intensity street lighting off West End Avenue. The lettering was too small to be read at a glance and beneath the lettering on the white card was imprinted a pale green shield. At a cursory glance it might pass for an official identification card. He put everything back in the wallet and slid the ID card in so that it was exposed in the Plexigas window. Then he drove to the filling station.

It was a small one-man station with a single lube rack; the proprietor was squirting grease up into the fittings of a Cadillac elevated on the lift. Paul stood just inside the stall and waited for the mechanic to notice him.

The mechanic lowered the grease gun and glanced at him. "Help you, mister?"

"I'm looking for a man named Orson Pyne. Lives a couple of blocks down here. Thought you might know him."

"Well I might."

Paul flashed the wallet, opening it to show the card inside the plastic window. "It's official."

The mechanic lowered the grease gun; his face changed. "What's it about?"

"Just a routine inquiry. Pyne lives in that brown and white house in the middle of the third block down there, does he?"

191

"Aeah, he does."

"He have his car serviced here?"

"Yes, he's been a regular customer a long time now."

"Is he a family man?"

"What is this, some kind of credit investigation?"

"I'm afraid I'm not at liberty to say."

"Well he used to be a family man. Wife died a few years ago, lung cancer I think. He's got a kid, just about grown up now I guess. Doesn't live at home anyhow."

"So Pyne lives alone."

"Yes sir. He's a quiet kind of guy."

"Pays his bills regularly?"

"He's real reliable, yes sir. Takes real good care of his car too. Sometimes that means something about a person, don't it?"

"It does, yes. What kind of car does he drive?"

"Seventy-two Ambassador. A real cream puff."

"You look after it for him, do you?"

"Well once in a while he takes it back to the American Motors place. You know, the big servicings, twenty-four thousand mile stuff. But I do all the routine work for him. He's real conscientious about oil changes and all that stuff. I just wish more of my customers would—"

"Do you happen to know where Mr. Pyne works?"

"Sure, don't you? He teaches college over at the university. Chemistry, biology, something like that."

"What time does he usually get home?"

"Well I couldn't tell you that, Mister. I don't keep tabs on nobody. Sometimes I see him, he stops in here on his way home, it's different times different days. You know how it is with teachers. But if you want to talk to him he ought to be home by suppertime I guess."

"Thanks very much for your help. I'd appreciate it if

you'd keep it under your hat. We wouldn't want to upset him for no reason. I mean everything seems to check out, there's no reason to worry Mr. Pyne."

"No sir, I can see that all right."

"Thanks again." Paul went back to his car.

38

IN THE LIBRARY he looked up Orson Pyne in the university catalogue. Pyne was forty-seven, an assistant professor in the Physics Department. He had a B.S. from the University of Oklahoma, an M.S. from Cal Tech and a Ph.D. from Northwestern, the latter acquired in 1968. He was one of the five authors of a basic physics textbook used by freshmen. He had served in the Navy from 1947 to 1953. A four-year hitch extended by the Korean War, evidently. There wasn't anything else about him. Paul tried various editions of *Who's Who* but Pyne wasn't listed in any of them.

He drove back to Reba Place and staked himself out a few doors away from Pyne's house. He still didn't know that he'd found his man; it seemed too easy; as the afternoon dragged by he thought of all the possibilities and was ready to conclude it was a blind alley. Truett's .45 Luger hadn't been the only one in the world. And it seemed too coincidental to be possible that both vigilantes had armed themselves from the same gun shop. Truett's was one of a hundred gun shops beyond the state line and it didn't advertise in the Chicago papers.

But the .45 Luger, if not unique, was very rare and he remembered something Truett had said that first time he'd been there: *Far as I know this is the only one like it this side of Los Angeles.* Even if he'd been exaggerating its rarity it still made Orson Pyne a possibility. . . .

Factors for-and-against kept warring in his mind but in the end he knew it didn't matter; Pyne was the only lead he had. If it turned out Pyne wasn't the second vigilante then he had nothing else to try. He'd have to give it up. He'd had one piece of information the police hadn't had —Truett and the Luger—and since it was the only advantage he had, he was pressing it. There was no point worrying now about whether it would pay off.

Five o'clock went by before the green Ambassador turned into the driveway. It stopped there, not proceeding back to the carport, and on that evidence Paul suspected Pyne intended to go out again. From his car he watched the man emerge from the car and walk up the porch steps. A tall man, lean with a scholar's stoop; dark hair combed sidewise across the high forehead; a thin face, almost a satyr's face. His appearance was hardly sinister.

But then neither is mine.

Full darkness came only a few minutes later. Lights came on in the back of the house—the kitchen? The front windows remained dark. Paul slipped on his rubber gloves and opened the dimestore package of fluorescent red tape. He tore off two arm's-length strips of it and quietly left his car trailing the gummed tape from his fingertips.

Down the block a car arrived home and Paul waited until its driver parked and went inside a house. Then he walked to Pyne's car and swiftly pressed the tape across the rear

195

bumper. He straightened and went directly back to his own car. The fluorescent tape would make it easier to follow Pyne at a distance in the night; Pyne probably wouldn't notice it and even if he did there was no harm in it for Paul.

At seven a man came out of Pyne's door and descended the steps. At first Paul was confused. The man had pale hair —grey or blond—and a long pale mustache. Then he realized it was Pyne in wig and false whiskers. It made him smile a bit. Pyne backed the Ambassador out of the driveway and rolled toward Paul. When the Ambassador had disappeared at the corner by the filling station, Paul made a quick U-turn and followed.

It was easy tailing the bright strip of red tape. He hung back more than a block, letting traffic intervene. Was it going to be this easy?

There was a shopping center on the right and the Ambassador turned into its parking lot. Paul slowed as he went past, and cramped the car into the second entrance to the lot. He cruised through the lanes—most of the stores were still open and there were hundreds of cars.

Pyne had pulled into a slot at the far end of the lot. Paul reached the end of a row, went around the parked cars and started slowly up the next row; through the glass of the cars he watched Pyne. The tall man got out of the Ambassador and locked it. Did he have some secret knowledge of a crime planned here in this parking lot?

Then Pyne went into his pocket and brought something out. It was too small to be visible; certainly not a gun. He walked across the aisle between parking rows and looked all around him. Paul turned and came driving toward him down the aisle. Pyne stooped, fitting his key into the lock of a battered old car.

He's changing cars.

How brilliant, he thought. *It's something I should have thought of.*

It was at least ten years old—the kind of car you could buy for a hundred dollars cash with no questions asked. A phony name, a phony address. Untraceable.

Pyne was backing the old car out. Paul gave it close scrutiny as he drove past. It was pocked with dents and rust stains; it squatted low on its springs. It was a four-door Impala; it had once been blue but had faded toward grey. It had a Wisconsin plate. He recognized the deep treads of the snow tires: Pyne wasn't taking chances on getting stuck. Probably the car was in much better mechanical shape than the exterior implied; Pyne was a physicist, he'd have a respect for mechanical things and an awareness of the need for maintenance to ensure reliability. But it was a sure thing he didn't have it serviced in that filling station where he took the Ambassador.

Well of course he was clever. He'd have been caught long ago otherwise.

But if that was the case why had he used his own name and address when he'd bought the Luger from Truett? And why the Luger at all, since it was so rare and easily identifiable?

It was a question to which he couldn't provide an answer out of pure speculation. Possibly when Pyne had bought the gun he hadn't had vigilantism in mind; perhaps that had come afterward. There were a lot of ifs and none of them really mattered; the only thing that mattered was the answer to one question: was Pyne the other Vigilante?

He knew how to force Pyne to cease his raids. But he couldn't confront Pyne until he was absolutely certain Pyne was the right man. Confront an innocent man and the whole thing could backfire in his face: an innocent man

197

would have no reason not to turn Paul in to the police. Only the second vigilante could be counted on to keep Paul's secret.

He followed the Impala south into Chicago.

Ω

39

HE SAW another reason why Pyne had chosen the dilapidated old car: it blended into the neighborhoods Pyne liked to prowl. Nobody was likely to mistake it for an unmarked official car.

It fascinated him to watch the way Pyne worked: it was as if he himself had trained the man. Pyne tried twice to entice muggers to follow him out of night-service pawnshops on the South Side. When that failed he parked the car on a side street and went into a bar and fifteen minutes later came stumbling out, patently drunk, and went wandering in search of his car. No one trailed him. Pyne was perfectly sober when he got in the car and drove away.

Paul gave him a one-block lead.

In the back streets of the ghetto Pyne drove at a crawl, searching the shadows. Paul had to take risks, veering away and driving around a block and waiting for Pyne to go by in front of him; otherwise Pyne would have realized a car was dogging him. He seemed preoccupied with his own hunt and Paul saw no indication that he was worried about surveillance but there was no point making his presence obvious.

Paul reached under the car seat. He pulled out both of his guns; slipped the Centennial in his right coat pocket and the .25 automatic in his left. He had to get rid of them tonight. He had the cleaning kit under the seat as well. He knew where he'd get rid of them, on his way home.

The Impala made a right turn into a dark narrow passage. Paul turned right a block earlier and went quickly along the parallel street to the corner, and looked left, waiting for the Impala to appear a block away.

It took too long; the car still didn't show up. Paul made the left and drove to the corner.

It was there, stopped in the middle of the passage; the lights were off. In the darkness it was hard to make things out but he saw the car door open slowly. The interior light did not go on; evidently it had been disconnected. A shadow emerged from the car—vaguely he could see Pyne's light-colored wig. And the hard silhouette of the gun in Pyne's hand.

Pyne's head was thrown back; he was looking at the upper windows of a four-story brick tenement. Paul turned everything off—ignition and lights—and let the car roll silently through the intersection to the far side. When it stopped he set the emergency brake, got out and walked back to the corner.

Pyne had his back to Paul. He stood on the sidewalk looking up at the building across the street from him. Paul began to walk forward, not hurrying.

He'd seen what he had to see: the gun in Pyne's hand. It was confirmation enough.

Pyne heard him coming. Casually the gun-hand went into

the coat pocket and with the other hand Pyne reached inside and brought out a cigarette. Then to screen his lighter from the wind he turned and hunched, and the maneuver enabled him to peek at Paul.

The tall man saw it wasn't a cop and Paul saw his shoulders relax. Paul glanced up at the building Pyne had been staring at. There was a light moving around behind a window up there—a flashlight, probably. Pyne had keen eyes.

And from where he was standing he commanded an upward view of the outside fire escape of the building.

Paul stopped ten feet away and spoke softly. "Let's let him get away with it this time, what do you say."

The tall man stared at him.

"Your name's Orson Pyne," Paul told him, "and that's a forty-five caliber Luger in your right hand coat pocket."

"Who the hell are you?"

"If you ever use that Luger again I'll have to give the police your name. That's all I'll need to tell them. They'll find the rest themselves. It's got to stop, Mr. Pine. It's no good, it didn't work, it was wrong. You can't just—"

Pyne had very fast reactions. Paul saw the right hand lift from the coat pocket and he didn't have to wait and find out Pyne's intentions; he had time only to throw himself to the side, diving behind Pyne's Impala, and the noise was earsplitting when the first hollow-point .45 slug smashed the fender of the car above him.

Paul skidded on the frozen surface, abrading his right side; he drew his legs up foetally to get them out of the line of fire; he heard Pyne's feet moving and he jabbed his hand desperately into his coat pocket. He lay on his right side; it was his left hand and that was the little automatic, the .25, and it felt absurdly toylike in his hand.

The Luger exploded again and the bullet screamed off the pavement; he heard it slam the bricks across the road.

Paul dropped flat. Beneath the car he saw the shadows of the tall man's overshoes, moving hesitantly. Paul fired.

Left-handed; it was a miss; the bullet whined off the curb. The overshoes began to run toward the car.

Terror pumped adrenaline through him; his hand shook. He rolled back into the street and that was what took Pyne by surprise because Pyne expected him to cling to the shelter of the car. Paul came in sight before Pyne expected it and when Pyne fired it was too hasty; the shot went wide somewhere and Paul was shooting as fast as he could pull trigger, the sounds reverberating madly in the narrow canyon like something careening around inside a metal can.

The .25's stopped Pyne in his tracks and hurled him backward, exploding against his body; the Luger fired once more, high into the air; then the tall man toppled. It was clear by the way he fell that he was dead: one of the wild bullets had struck his throat.

"Dear God."

Ω

40

PEOPLE WOULD HAVE HEARD the noise but they wouldn't have a fix on it and it wasn't the kind of place where things were reported immediately to the Man. He glanced at the upper windows; the moving light had been extinguished. Certainly that one wasn't going to report anything.

It came to him then in a moment's crazy inspiration as he crawled to his feet and stood swaying. He felt an insistent hammering behind his eyes. It would work; he saw it full-blown in his mind and he was incredulous.

He took the Centennial from his pocket. He still wore the rubber gloves. He knelt by the dead man. The Luger was clutched in the outflung right hand. Paul slipped the Centennial into Pyne's left-hand coat pocket. Then he went back to his own car. He had a bad moment of shakes before he was able to turn the key but he knew he had to get clear before he could afford to let the reaction hit him and he forced himself, tightening up the muscles of his stomach and squeezing the steering wheel with all his strength until the dizziness subsided. He gunned the car away and didn't put the headlights on until he was several blocks distant. He heard the approaching sirens but he never saw them; he stayed to the side streets until he was well away.

Then he parked and let himself slump with the back of his head on top of the seat-back, choking down the nausea and letting the shock wash over him, not fighting it, waiting it out.

There was still one thing to do. When he felt strong enough he started the car again and drove north into the Loop. It was nearly two in the morning; the city was dark and silent. He went north onto the Dearborn Avenue bridge and stopped the car in the middle of the bridge. Put the .25 automatic into the paper bag along with the gun-cleaning kit and stepped out of the car. He stopped briefly, his nerves prey to imagined dangers, but nothing stirred in the night and he took two quick strides to the railing and dropped the heavy bag into the Chicago River.

Then he drove home.

Ω

41

¶ CHICAGO, JAN. 7TH—The Chicago vigilante is dead. He died as he lived, by the gun.

The body of Orson B. Pyne, 47, of 2806 Reba Place, Evanston, was found last night riddled with bullets in a side street off Lafayette Avenue in South Chicago after police received two telephone reports that shots had been heard in the area.

(For story on Pyne's background, see page 14.)

Found in the dead man's possession were a .45 caliber Luger automatic pistol and a .38 S&W Centennial revolver. The Luger had been fired four times, according to the police. The Centennial had not been fired.

Pyne was killed by several shots from a small-caliber weapon, according to Captain Victor Mastro of the Chicago Police Department's special Vigilante Squad.

Mastro said, "He finally ran into a criminal who was faster than he was."

Police are searching for the man who killed Pyne but if there are clues to his identity, the police are not revealing them. Captain Mastro said, "He was found on a very dark side street. Probably he went in there to entice a mugger to follow him. The mugger was armed —preliminary ballistics reports indicate it was probably a .25 caliber automatic with dum-dum bullets—and evidently there was a gunfight. The entry angle of the death bullets indicates that the assailant was flat on the street when he fired, which may mean he'd ducked for cover or may mean he was wounded himself, although we doubt that's the case, since any injury from that .45 Luger would have torn him up pretty badly and he wouldn't have gotten away. We found no blood on the scene that couldn't be traced to the dead man."

Both guns found in Pyne's possession were rushed immediately to the police laboratory.Captain Mastro said, "There's absolutely no doubt that these are the two weapons that were used in all the vigilante cases."

Ω

42

A WEEK LATER he left the office at six o'clock and put the Pontiac up Lake Shore Drive through a gentle snowfall; he was at Harry Chisum's house by half past the hour.

He'd stopped by two days ago but Irene's car had been parked at the curb and he'd gone by without stopping; he'd had a very bad time of it that night but he knew he had to face the old man and it was better to get it done.

There was no sign of Irene's car. He rang the doorbell and took a vague satisfaction in the surprise with which Harry Chisum greeted him.

"I'd like to talk to you."

"By all means, Paul. Come in."

"Are you alone? I don't want to disturb—"

"We're quite alone." Harry led him into the parlor and Paul glanced at the ancient television set. Not long ago he'd have hated it for betraying him.

"Would you like a drink? Sherry perhaps?"

"Scotch if you've got it."

"How are things at Childress Associates?"

"They keep me jumping."

"It's probably good for you to have a lot of work to do."

"Yes, it's a life saver."

Harry made the drinks and they returned to the parlor. "Well then."

Paul said, "There's something I want you to know."

"I've pretty much figured it out for myself."

"I tried to talk to him. He wouldn't let me finish. He pulled out that goddamned Luger and started shooting at me. It was blind luck as much as anything else. It might just as easily have been me. I had no intention of shooting the man, Harry."

"Yes."

"I've got to know you believe that."

"Is there any reason why I shouldn't?"

"When I planted the thirty-eight on his body it was an afterthought. I hadn't planned that."

"All right, Paul."

"If he'd only listened to me I could have talked him out of it. It would have worked."

"He was an impatient man, I suppose. His son a heroin addict. . . ."

"He panicked, that's all."

"Yes."

"Harry, I get a feeling you don't believe me."

"Why shouldn't I?"

Paul looked down at his drink. "I don't deserve much consideration. I can't ask you to keep my secret. But I want you to believe this—it's important."

"Paul, I believe it. I'm utterly convinced you had no intention of killing that man. What more can I say to you?"

"You seem awfully listless."

"Have you listened to the radio today? Seen this afternoon's newspaper?"

"No. Why?"

Harry waved vaguely toward the table beyond the television set. There was a newspaper on it. "You'd better have a look."

Paul walked toward it. Behind him he heard the old man's voice: "We both thought it was ended. We didn't realize you'd started something that couldn't be stopped."

The headline slammed him in the eyes. He glanced at the columns beneath it. Phrases caught his eye: . . . *three separate incidents in the past forty-eight hours. . . . The same .32 caliber pistol appears to have been used in all three shootings. . . . Captain Victor Mastro was quoted as saying. . . . victims all had criminal records. . . .*

He stared in unbelief at the headline:

ANOTHER VIGILANTE?